PENGUIN BOOKS

The Scarecrow

Ronald Hugh Morrieson was born in Hawera, New
Zealand, in 1922, and lived there all his life. He earned
his living as a music teacher and musician, playing in
dance bands throughout South Taranaki. Morrieson
died in 1972. His other novels are *Came a Hot Friday*,
Predicament and *Pallet on the Floor*.

NEW ZEALAND POPULAR PENGUINS

THE SCARECROW

RONALD HUGH MORRIESON

PENGUIN BOOKS

PENGUIN BOOKS

Published by the Penguin Group

Penguin Group (NZ), 67 Apollo Drive, Rosedale,
North Shore 0632, New Zealand (a division of Pearson New Zealand Ltd)
Penguin Group (USA) Inc., 375 Hudson Street,
New York, New York 10014, USA
Penguin Group (Canada), 90 Eglinton Avenue East, Suite 700, Toronto,
Ontario, M4P 2Y3, Canada (a division of Pearson Penguin Canada Inc.)
Penguin Books Ltd, 80 Strand, London, WC2R 0RL, England
Penguin Ireland, 25 St Stephen's Green,
Dublin 2, Ireland (a division of Penguin Books Ltd)
Penguin Group (Australia), 250 Camberwell Road, Camberwell,
Victoria 3124, Australia (a division of Pearson Australia Group Pty Ltd)
Penguin Books India Pvt Ltd, 11, Community Centre,
Panchsheel Park, New Delhi – 110 017, India
Penguin Books (South Africa) (Pty) Ltd, 24 Sturdee Avenue,
Rosebank, Johannesburg 2196, South Africa

Penguin Books Ltd, Registered Offices: 80 Strand, London, WC2R 0RL,
England

First published by Angus & Robertson Ltd, 1963
This edition published by Penguin Group (NZ), 2010
1 3 5 7 9 10 8 6 4 2

Printed in Australia by McPherson's Printing Group

ISBN 9780143205999

A catalogue record for this book is available
from the National Library of New Zealand.

www.penguin.co.nz

Chapter One

THE SAME WEEK our fowls were stolen, Daphne Moran had her throat cut.

Big dunce that I was at school, my essays, if not my spelling, used to be thought quite good, and I was a keen reader, which is probably why I now presume to set myself up as the chronicler of Klynham's hour in the limelight. This was certainly the most hectic and the darkest chapter in the whole history of the town and, just like I have heard said "Murder will out", it seems to me that the true story is bursting to be told sooner or later. It may be that I am biting off more than I can chew in tackling the job, but who, I ask myself, is going to come to light if I do not accept the challenge? Who was more constantly mixed up in every scene than little me? But nobody! And whose family knew more of any ins and outs that I may have missed myself than my own family? Echo answers whose!

So it looks like it is over to me to go ahead and, in retrospect, piece together the entire grisly and dramatic episode. Nearly all should turn out to be a genuine blow-by-blow account. Some of it will have been told to me, of course, and some extra elusive bits and pieces may force me to use my imagination; but surely I get some licence if I am really going to blow the top off that strange affair at last. Grant me a little licence, then, is my plea.

1

In *Treasure Island* I liked the sound of "The same broadside I lost my leg, Old Pew lost his deadlights." When I get around to writing myself, I decided, that is how I am going to sound. It is harder than it looks. The opening sentence of my story is as near as I can get.

The two crimes, the one so trivial and the other so diabolical, do belong to the same story, but only because a young girl took a newspaper from her aunt's basket, and a man whose every breath was a whiff of brimstone thought he was haunted. Klynham is two hundred and fifty miles from the city. In the city the trams clanged and the newsboys shouted; the autumn dusk was ruddy with the glare of lights. In our little town a horse would clip-clop along the dead centre of the main street at noonday; at nightfall, the lights from kitchens shone out over back-yards, and the street lamps which glimmered into life were few and far between. There was a street lamp outside our tumbledown house and the moths it attracted looked as big as bats.

The name is Poindexter. It is a rather impressive name, I have always thought, and yet we were just about the most no-account outfit in the town. This is the voice of Edward Clifton (Neddy) of the Poindexter ilk and I should know.

The trouble with the Poindexters was ready cash and Athol Cudby. We had no ready cash to speak of, but we had stacks of Athol Claude Cudby. It has long been my contention that the constant presence of that man had a more degrading influence on our household than any other factor.

Apparently, while the slump was playing fortissimo and I was playing cowboys and Indians, we became locally celebrated for not paying the rent, chopping up partitions for fuel against the wintry blasts, boozy parties, and the girls getting into the time-honoured spot of bother. Both Winifred and Constance got married the bumpy way and these things take living down in a place the size of Klyn-

2

ham. We also had quarrels. We lived in a whole series of houses and every one of them had a window, or windows, with a large star in the glass because somebody ducked. The house on the corner of Smythe and Winchester Streets, which is where we were living in the early autumn of this memorable, nay, unforgettable, year, featured two such windows. However, by this time, things were brightening a little. We had a good-natured, easy-going landlord, and money was not playing quite so hard to get. There was even some talk of taking the owner up on his offer, paying a higher rent and making the old shack our own. Things were looking up, but we still had Uncle Athol.

Uncle Athol is a bludger, a prize bludger, the soft voiced, "thank-yuh-kindly", hat-touching type whose answer to flood, famine and plague is a mackintosh. If Athol C. Cudby ever whipped up a bead of honest sweat in his whole life I would appreciate finding out just where and when in order to send it to Ripley. It is not a bit of use telling me it was losing an eye that soured him against toil, because he had both his eyes right up to the time when, strictly from hunger, he undertook to go on a fencing contract somewhere in the back of beyond, with two cronies. First time up he took a blind swipe at a post with a hammer; and a piece of No. 8 fencing wire promptly took a swipe back and scored a Lord Nelson. On the strength of his glass eye (whoever matched that fishy eye was a craftsman and is almost certainly still whistling for the price) Uncle Athol has been known to attend an Anzac Day parade wearing an army overcoat he got from "Clem's Wardrobe", an establishment now liquidated on account of greater universal prosperity. Consider a man, who has never been closer to the army than a secondhand overcoat, attending a sacred ceremony like an Anzac Day parade just for the booze he can get out of it. This will serve to illustrate his attitude and lack of principle.

3

"Bull's wool rules the world" is his motto and sometimes I am inclined to think he could be right. He certainly seems to have pulled the wool over a lot of eyes in this town in his time. When I was just a kid he had me bluffed too, but those days are gone.

Uncle Athol took a great interest in the hen-coop Leslie Wilson and I built when we got bitten by the poultry bug. Les was a great buddy of mine in those days when we were in short pants. We went collecting cones from pine plantations weekend after weekend, tore our pants on barbed-wire fences, fell in creeks and fell out of trees and braved all manner of hazards, including being bitten by dogs, when we hawked the pine-cones from door to door, and all to buy half a dozen Black Orpington fowls, which the auctioneer said were pullets. Looking back with a certain sourness, it is my contention that the auctioneer used the term "pullets" the way a drunk would yell out "Hi girls" to a busload of grandmothers on a conducted tour; but, be that as it may, those chooks belonged to Les and me and when we found a brown egg in the coop which Uncle Athol had given us advice on how to build, to say we were walking on air is to be guilty of withholding the true facts. Saturday morning Les turned up with a book on poultry farming and now it did not seem as if anything was going to prevent us making a fortune.

"There sure musta been fowls around for some time," I said, looking through the book, which had no cover and seemed to be written in copperplate on parchment. At a glance it might have been a first edition Chaucer. " 'Stonishin' to think of 'em having fowls way back when like this."

"Don'tcha worry yuh head over that," said Les, reclaiming the book. "There weren't too many flies on these old-timers. This old geezer here with the beard musta known fowls like the palm of his hand to write this book. Way I look at it, with a book like this to refer to and study, we'd

4

just be wasting our time going on to the Tec. With a book like this and the super strain of fowls like we managed to get for a kick off, there just isn't any point in wasting our energy on anything else. We'll be able to retire and just spechlize in breeding before we're any age at *tall*."

"Seems funny those chooks are still in the box at the back at this hour," I said, poking a stick through the wire-netting. "Seems like they're sleeping in pretty late for a Saturday."

We were so dumb in those days it was ten minutes or thereabouts before we got anxious enough to investigate. Les's bottom jaw fell so low, I thought maybe he was going to eat the handful of black feathers which was all we found.

Chord in E minor, please, maestro.

Well, there was only one crowd that was capable of a crime of this magnitude and that was the Victor Lynch boys. We both thought the same thing at the same time, but neither of us mentioned the dread name. In the end Les beckoned me to follow him and when he finally stopped down by the rhubarb, he said, "Victor Lynch."

I remember we sold our remaining sack of pine-cones that morning and we went to see a Hopalong Cassidy in the afternoon. We walked slowly and purposefully, loosely, ready to reach for our guns at the drop of a hat, speaking only in condensed, staccato bursts, these men are dangerous.

While we were in the theatre watching the screen grimly, Uncle Athol was raffling those fowls, twenty tickets a time, sixpence a knock, in the Federal Hotel. Whenever I hear that song, "I'll be Glad When You're Dead, You Rascal You", I think of that man.

Theatre is dignifying Klynham's cinema somewhat. It was a big draughty barn of a place, but many happy hours we spent therein. The building has had a great face-lift recently, but I recall it fondly the way it was in the days

5

when Les and I sat enthralled by a serial picture called "The King of Diamonds", and the kids stamped on the floor and whistled at each certificate of approval, unless it was a travel film and then they hooted and groaned. There was always a chance of my bare arm brushing against the electrically charged flesh of Josephine Mc-Clinton again as we crowded down the stairs at interval, or even maybe, some day, fluking a seat alongside her. There were big pictures of Tom Mix and Robert Montgomery and Dolores Del Rio and young Jane Withers on the walls of the stairway. My crush on Josephine was top-secret stuff, but Les and I openly admitted that we thought Jane Withers was a bit of all right, even if she did have a double chin. It was only puppy fat, Les reckoned.

After the flicks, Les and I cut out what was left of the cone money on a milk-shake. We took our time and there were not many people left hanging around when we came out from the soda fountain. We walked the length of the main street and we met Prudence.

At one end, the cinema end, of the main street, is a band rotunda into which people throw the paper off fish and chips. At the other end is a giant elm-tree fenced off with wrought-iron railing. These two features of Klynham stare along the middle of the main street at each other in the frustrated but resigned manner of pensioned-off cannons in a park. The sun rises behind the elm-tree and sets behind the band rotunda, its slanting rays at sundown imparting to this edifice a minaret-like appearance. At the western end are not only the band rotunda and the cinema, but also the billiard saloon. My big brother, Herbert, spent more time at the billiard saloon than he did up at our house on the corner of Smythe and Winchester Streets. On Sundays, Herbert hung around the house and talked about the billiard saloon and people called Kelly and Jack Glenn and Hodson. The other end of the main street was, and still is, popular with the farmers on market days. They used to park their Dodge tourers around the big elm-tree and sit on the running boards, or on the leaf-strewn, shadow-dappled grass and eat pies.

On the main street were two butchers' shops with sawdust on the floors and one of these sold the finest sausages in the world it was generally understood. The other butcher had the best steak. Everybody knew that this was so. There could be no gainsaying it. Even the children knew that one butcher was renowned for his sausages and the other for his steak, because they had heard it stated so often and so positively by their elders. This conflicting appeal to patronage could complicate shopping, but we were unaffected inasmuch as only the sausage master was willing to extend credit to the Poindexter family. We were resigned to gnawing away at the most gosh-awful steak. However, as Ma said, "What yuh lose on the swings yuh get on the rouseabouts." Good old Ma! There were several confectionery shops with counters and tables for sundae and milk-shake consumers, a chemist, a saddlery, ironmongery, two grocery shops, two banks, and an old-established drapery business. Dabney's, the undertaking and furnishing business, half-way along the street, was a very old-established firm, but it was shut as often as not; either that or there was no answer, and people never went there to buy furniture. They went to Hardley & Manning.

Hardley & Manning was our really big store and no shopping expedition was complete without using it as a short cut between two streets. The adventure of going right through Hardley & Manning, using it as a short cut, never palled. One emerged on a wide, dusty back street which commanded a fine view of the misty hinterland. It also featured the defunct Jubilee Hotel. There were three other hotels at Klynham, a number said by some to be ridiculous for the population while others bemoaned the days when there were four, before they shut down the

Jubilee. Too many pubs or not, the big-bellied licensees, who wheezed masterfully in those open doorways were recognized as men of affluence, but they certainly spent no money having the litter swept up from the bare corridors between the bars. Except for the hotels, such two-storeyed buildings as the street boasted were unoccupied upstairs and some even had the top windows boarded up.

The main street always looked desolate at this hour on a Saturday as most of the shops closed at mid-day. Walking late on a Saturday afternoon the only person one could ever really count on meeting was Sam Finn, the local halfwit, another attraction Klynham ran to in those days. Poor Sam Finn. When I think of him I feel as if I am looking back at the town through the wrong end of a telescope. And it feels odd to reflect that I, alone, probably hold the key to the secret of his disappearance, even the secret of his grave. But Sam Finn and the equally ill-fated Mabel Collinson, the music teacher, part and parcel of this story as they may be, will have to wait their cue. As I said the main street of Klynham looked desolate this Saturday after the cinema had closed. There was a sniff of dark smoke from the railway station in the air. The afternoon seemed reproachfully old. I would not have even seen Prudence who was diagonally across the intersection from us, I was still so burnt up about the raid, but Les nudged me and said, "That's yuh sister, Ned."

We stopped only because Les stopped, and Prudence came across the street slowly, shielding her eyes from the westering sun. When she reached the shadow of the big elm-tree her squint became an engaging grin. She was two years older than me and she always looked to me as if she had a dirty face, but I realize now that everybody must have been right when they said she was "real pretty". I think everybody was downright puzzled too at one of the Poindexter girls turning out a beauty, because no one else I can recall in the family was any oil painting.

One night there was a big party at our house on the corner of Winchester and Smythe Streets and it finished up with the usual donnybrook and some drunk said, "Yuh all pretty stuck up about that Pru being so pretty loike, but it's my opinion someone come over the wall." Another window got christened and you could say the party was over, except for a lot of mumbling and swearing around the house and out in the street too. I tried to figure out what this remark meant, but I dozed off without solving the riddle. I was glad the party was over, so I could get a little shuteye.

I guess I was pretty dumb in those days. I can see now Leslie Wilson must have been really smitten with Prudence, though he would have died sooner than let on. Sometimes I even wonder if she might have been the main attraction for Les around at our place and not his old buddy, me, at all.

In the dead of night (9.30 or thereabouts) Les and I carried out reprisals and struck as mortal a blow as we could muster at the Victor Lynch empire. Lynch was the master-mind behind much evil in the juvenile underworld at Klynham, so justice was again working along mysterious ways to hit the bull's eye, but the fact remains, Uncle Athol's criminal duplicity put Les and me in a nasty spot. Only a seething sense of outrage could have given us the courage to move in on gang-leader Lynch the way we did that Saturday night. The well-known expression "taking your life in your hands" hardly meets the case. It would be more apt to liken it to putting your life in the hip pocket of your pants and going roller skating. Victor Lynch cast a big loop in our little world. Ironically I remember hearing Uncle Athol's drunken snoring as I crept out of the house.

It was what I always think of as a soft sort of night, warm and dark with a velvety breeze kicking the moonbeams around, and a cannon fired down Smythe Street

9

would not have startled a tom-cat. Les was leaning on a garage doorway half-way along and he fell into step with me without saying a word, real secret-service stuff. He had a big bundle stuffed under his arm, so I knew he had remembered to bring the sacks along, as planned. I could have easily grabbed one myself on the way out, but Ma would have missed a sack off the kitchen floor in a jiffy. Ma was a great one for appearances. I honestly believe if the menfolk of the house had shaken their ideas up a bit, Ma could have made things really shipshape.

Only veterans of such underhand, nocturnal activity will sympathize with how conspicuous we felt as we moved in on our target that night. In theory, sneaking up on the benighted Lynch home seemed as easy as falling off a log, but it got trickier and trickier. All the points we had imagined to be in our favour turned against us. For example, Lynch's house being on the outskirts of Klynham where the houses thinned out, we found only made us greater objects of suspicion. The street lamps were just as numerous as in the heart of the town, but the bitumen on the roads and footpaths gave out to loose gravel and our footfalls kicked up a row like a stonecrusher.

When we were opposite the drive at the side of Lynch's house we crouched down for a trembling moment and then made a stooping dash for it. There were two concrete strips for the car, but, in between and at the sides, were strips of lawn which helped. The drive was right beside the house and the going under the high, lighted window on finger-tips and tiptoe was murder. My heart was kicking the sides out of my neck. As soon as we reached the lawn at the back of the house we made another dash for the garden and the shelter of the hedge. We were in. But no one was more aware than I of the fact that we were not out again and safe.

Les was leading the way because he was delivery boy for his father some Saturday mornings and, standing on

Lynch's back porch, he had spied out the land for no real reason, except that this was enemy territory. His curiosity was paying off now. It was pitch dark, but Les took me right to the fowlhouse door. The fowlhouse had been built just where the garden began to fall away steeply down into a deep gully. It was a real job, not just a poor old coop like we had built. It was not very high or deep, but it seemed about twenty feet long and was stoutly built of timber and corrugated iron. There was a big bolt on the door, but no padlock.

The bolt creaked as Les drew it; a fowl made a sound something like Uncle Athol between snores; we froze for a moment, and then stepped inside smartly. We half-shut the door behind us quickly, but not quickly enough to beat the creaking hinges. The fowls clucked sleepily. We stood like statues.

Les nudged me. I took the sacks. We had this worked out like a bank robbery. With one sack under my arm I held the other wide open with both hands. Les took my arm and I stepped up close behind him as he groped nearer the perch. The fowls seemed to have dismissed the sounds of our presence as just cats or something, and be dozing off again, and for the first time I really began to think we were going to get away with it. In a lot of books I had read, I had noticed that the hero or heroine felt an insane desire to giggle. Right then I knew just how they felt.

When I heard the first fowl going into the sack, I heard Les snigger and I gritted my teeth and made a sort of sizzling noise through my nose like a slow leak.

"Shut up, yuh bastids," said Les. The agitation along the perch was spreading.

"Next bag," he hissed.

"Hang on, hang on."

I could see his outline clearly now, as I gathered the top of the sack together and whipped the string tight. A

11

fowl jumped down and scuttled around, somnolently hysterical. I propped the first sack against the wire-netting and stumbled after Les with the next wide open. By now the noise in the fowlhouse was in the uproar category. A huge fowl flew into our faces, giant wings beating.

"That's it; let's go."

"C'mon, we're gone."

When we were outside the door, we saw the torchlight coming down the garden path. I fled down into the gully. I was carrying the second sack, which was only half-full. Les told me he went along the back of the fowlhouse and over the fence into the neighbour's yard. He went down the path to the street and lit out into a four-minute mile, sack over shoulder and all. I should have gone with him. It must have taken me twenty minutes to cover three hundred yards of gully bed. A blow-by-blow account of my travail in that virgin gully is to be avoided at all costs. Only three out of six big, strapping fowls survived the journey. Whether they drowned, suffocated or just plain had their brains beaten out is anybody's guess. At last, exhausted, via swampy, never-used lanes, watched by spooky trees, I reached our secret hide-out in Fitzherbert's shed.

There had been eleven fowls crammed into Les's sack. When I arrived they were dozing fitfully up on the old gig in the back corner of the big shed, like flooded-out campers billeted in a grandstand. Les had lit the candle, thereby summoning up a sinister gallery of hooded, bobbing figures to join the spiders around the walls.

I was drenched from head to toe and stiff with mud and blood. I stripped clean off and we washed every stitch of my clothes in the trough behind the shed. The night did not seem so warm, stark naked, but the breeze was velvet. The moon was in the gutter of the sky with its parking lights on and the pines grouped around the stile and along the fence between the paddock and the ruined Fitzherbert mansion were skinny old men leaning on their walking sticks.

We wrung the clothes out and hung them from rusty nails around the walls of the shed, and I went and sat in the pile of lucerne hay. Les and I had gone swimming in the "nuddy" time and time again, but it had never given me a feeling like this before, a feeling too delicious by far to be anything but evil. I wanted to make the feeling get worse, so I lit a cigarette, completely unconcerned whether tobacco stumped your growth or not. The school of thought which maintained tobacco stumped your growth was probably quite wrong anyway, I thought to myself. If you believed everything you read about what to eat and what not to eat, don't do this, don't do that, and you listened to everything every screwball told you, a guy was going to end up too scared to move, I reasoned.

Chapter Two

A WATERY solution of mist and sunlight grudgingly included Smythe Street in its early morning tour of inspection. It winced as it itemized, in a slapdash fashion, the rusty tin bath-tubs, stoves, lavatory pans, hot-water cylinders, etcetera, which cluttered up our yard behind the house. The square concrete building across the street from our tumbledown dwelling was fleetingly beautified with a lemon sheen. Soon it became possible to read the inexpertly painted inscription on the double doors of the big shed down at the end of our yard. D. H. POINDEXTER ANTIQUE DEALER AND VALUER. Although energetic efforts at erasion had been made it was also possible to discern in larger letters, DESERT HEAD FOR JUNK. We never found out who had the nerve to paint that derisive slogan on our shed. Actually the D. H. stood for Daniel Herbert. Some democratic birds began to bang snails on such parts of our roof as they considered in good enough shape to withstand the impact, and it could be said the business of seeing through another day had been officially opened.

Sunday was always a pretty grim morning for D. H. Poindexter (my old man) and my big brother Herbert, and Uncle Athol, but this Sunday I was right up with the field. While my eyelids were still at half-mast, recent events and the pending repercussions thereof hit me like a wet spade. Les and I had worked out every detail, but it took my subconscious mind to single out the key point of the whole manoeuvre. Hate and excitement can foul up anyone's judgment, but that old subconscious sure knows its onions. How, it said to me, spreading its hands pityingly, how in the name of God do you expect to get away with it? Victor Lynch takes your chooks Friday night and Saturday night you take his. Who else? Elementary, deah boy!

My clothes were steaming away on the end of the bed in the morning sun and I clambered into both of them. Someone leapt across the washhouse and held the door when I got there.

"It's me."

"Why don't yuh say?"

I went over to the tap and did my best to get what looked like plasticine to look like my hair again.

"Whatcha been up to?" asked Prudence, pulling her dress down.

"Mind yuh own business."

"Don't look at me in that tone of voice," Prudence said haughtily. "And please leave that seat up. There's too many one-armed drivers around this dump now and that's fuh sure."

She crossed to the tub, over which a cracked and spotted mirror was tacked to the wall, and combed her wealth of dark, gleaming hair. All along the window-sill were the discoloured butts of roll-your-owns the menfolk had put down while they were shaving. There were some matches on the copper and I debated whether I should have a quick smoke or not. I decided not. I was not so cocky this morning about this growth-stumping business. Rumour had it the Victor Lynch gang smoked like chimneys, but I had a sneaking desire to be a big guy some of these days.

About ten o'clock Les came around, looking surprisingly confident. We squatted down, down by the rhubarb, and I passed on my fears.

"I can't understand why we didn't see it that way yesterday, Les. Of course they'll cotton on to who did it. They took ours and we take theirs. We'll have to watch our step, boy, we're in for a bashing any day now."

"It might be more than that, Ned," said Les. "Old man Lynch'll call in the cops over this for cert."

My brain must have been addled on the Saturday not to think of these angles. We were right in the cart. It was only a matter of time.

Despite the shadow hanging over us, Sunday must have been a big day, romantically speaking, for Les Wilson, because Prudence came with us to the Fitzherbert shed where we headed automatically to discuss our predicament. It was the first time and I do not know now why we let her into the secret. Maybe we felt past caring or maybe Les worked it cunningly somehow, or she could have just latched on to us, but she came anyway. Prudence was a great scout and, although she thought we were a bit cracked, she played along with the way we hid behind hedges and kept doubling back to corners to make sure we were not being followed.

When we found eight or nine eggs in the shed Les and I were really rocked. I think we felt a bit small remembering our one brown egg.

"Just can't credit they lay like that all the time," Les said. "Maybe it's just nervus reactshun after last night."

I had a sinking feeling that we had betrayed a trust in letting Prudence know about the shed but I had to admit having her with us brightened us up. I still maintain she had a dirty face, but I was coming around gradually to admitting she was ornamental in her own way. She was full of fun and Les seemed a new man, so, in the end, I was getting quite perky myself and beginning to feel we might get away with the big fowl raid. Before long, what with some pears from the overgrown Fitzherbert orchard, and the last of the Ardath cigarettes, Les and I were right back to normal and planning how we would sell the eggs and use some of the money to buy wheat. Prudence was a full-blown member of the gang now with her arms around her legs and her chin on her knees and a lock of hair over one eye.

"Anyway all gangsters have molls," I said to Les, when we were in the orchard but Les was up a tree and said nothing.

The roof of the shed was at two different levels, but one of the lower beams ran the full width, as a brace, and from this it was possible to hang down and swing by the crook of one's knees. The beam was so roughly hewn it was almost round, but anyway Les and I had legs like iron. Nothing else for it, Prudence had to be in the act. She tried and tried to gather momentum to swing herself up over the beam, but she lacked the confidence and the knack of whipping the back muscles just at the right instant. We demonstrated the technique until I suspected I had strained my bowels. I excused myself and went and sat crabwise on the stile into the orchard. When I had been there some time, just staring at the back wall of the shed, I felt a compulsion to return. Prudence had stepped out of her skirt and, in tight, black knickers and blouse, was still attempting to swing over the beam. She just about had it mastered. In the end she did it. Prudence's legs were gorgeous, full, curving, dusky. Because she was my sister I was a real skeleton at the feast, but I began to get the same feeling I experienced sitting naked in the lucerne hay the night before.

The shed was windowless, twilit, musky. It was an odd feeling to emerge from it and find the noonday sun shining brightly and to realize it was not really late at all, only dinner-time.

When I reached home I missed Les's company and I began to feel unhappy and apprehensive again. I only

17

managed to shove down half a pork sausage at dinner-time, whereas I usually wolfed everything they gave me.

"You sick or something, boy?" said Prudence, spearing with her fork what I left on my plate and getting herself in consequence a dirty look from Uncle Athol. He always looked ten years older on a Sunday, because he skipped shaving and his bristles grew out white. He often left his teeth out on a Sunday too. Herbert had told me on the quiet that he reckoned Uncle Athol had got his teeth from Mr Dabney, the undertaker. Everyone said Mr Dabney was wealthy and sure enough he wore a collar and tie and had a gold watch, but when he got on the scoot he gravitated to characters like Athol C. Cudby and they stayed on the booze together for days. I am not certain whether Herbert had his facts straight, but sure enough it was after one of these jags with Mr Dabney that Uncle Athol appeared with teeth, and started acting in a superior way, putting on the dog a bit like Pop. Pop was a real character at putting on the dog, but it sort of came natural to him. Even when he was buying an old stove or hot-water cylinder, he contrived to act as if he were only looking such junk over to install it in the gatekeeper's lodge.

Uncle Athol gave out that he and Pop were partners in the buying and selling business, but Pop introduced him, when he could not get out of it, as "Mr Cudby, Mr Athol Cudby, my, hrrmp, contact man." I guess that just about sized him up too, always sniffing around on the trail of a yardful of junk somewhere; but, on account of his rupture, he never contacted anything heavy which he would have to heave up on the back of the truck. For the same reason he just stood around when Pop had to change a wheel, which amounted to a lot of standing time, the little old Dennis tip-truck having been known to throw three blowouts in three blocks. One of the standard topics of conversation was five-fifty by twenty-one tyres. If I live to be a hundred years old I am still going to hear voices yak yaking away about five-fifty twenty-ones.

"Great big pile of five-fifty twenty-ones yuh couldn't jump over. Been past there hundreds of times without dreaming—"

"I tell yuh it's a five-fifty twenty-one, spanking condition, been there for donkey's years. They'll never miss it."

"Pretty bald in places, but they're five-fifty twenty-ones awright."

"Been a minute earlier it 'ud been worth raking outa the fire. Coulda cried. 'Course it was a five-fifty twenty-one. Think a man doesn't—"

And so on.

In a way, I guess, five-fifty twenty-ones were the symbol of our sort of people. If the Poindexters ran to a coat of arms there would be a five-fifty twenty-one in one corner and a crank-handle in the other. Any automobile with a hint of streamlining had fat, well treaded, remote things referred to as six-hundred sixteens and that was the badge of the people on the other side of the wall.

The girl called Josephine McClinton had been produced by the people on the other side of the wall. Josephine was a blonde, whose smooth and shapely legs propelled a new bicycle down Smythe Street twice a week. I hid behind a stove when I saw her coming with her music case and through the grating I saw her look our junk yard over with a curious and scornful expression that wrung out my innards. She was definitely a six-hundred sixteener.

In the afternoon, Pop, blowing hard and red-faced from cranking the Dennis, shouted out at me over the noise of the engine, if I wanted to come with him on a trip. It was beginning to look as if something had prevented Les from coming around which left me at a loose end so I said "O.K."

Anyone who climbed up into the cab of our tip-truck found himself pretty high up in the world; but the horsehair sprouting out of the black leather seat and tickling your legs, and having to put one's feet on the fly-wheel housing because the floor boards were gone, and banging one's head on the roof every pothole, and having to yell out to be heard, were not aspects calculated to give one a superiority complex. I will admit here and now I was ashamed to bounce along in that old bomb and I was glad when I found we were heading out of town. Glad but worried.

"Where we headin', Pop?" I screamed.

"Te Rotiha," he roared.

"Te Rotiha? Yuh nuts! It's miles and miles. We'll never make it, we'll never get back."

Pop now set out on a long harangue about the merits of the Dennis and how it would not be the official vehicle of the firm of Dee-aitch Poindexter if it were not and so on and so on, and how over the years it had etc., etc., and despite what ignorant people said ad infinitum, ad nauseam . . . I only heard a word here and there. I had only been as far afield as Te Rotiha once before so I consoled myself reflecting that a guy really ought to travel if he ever wanted to speak on different topics with any authority and, also, as Ma was wont to point out, while I was doing this I wasn't doing anybody else out of anything. But I was pleased and surprised when we actually got to Te Rotiha all the same, as it must have been the best part of twelve miles from Klynham.

There is just a chance that if I had not gone on that hazardous bump-bottom journey that Sunday afternoon this tale would not have been told. As we turned off the crossroads I glimpsed, for the first time, the sinister man.

The Dennis ground its way in low gear down to the station yard and Pop and I exchanged a quick look. Pop was bursting with conceit and trying to hide it. I was beginning to feel a bit proud about the old heap of nuts and bolts myself but as we crossed the railway lines behind the train that was being made-up on the back line I heard the explosion I had been waiting for the whole trip. If there was one word that was completely taboo at home it was the one Pop shouted out at this juncture. I was not too sure what made it such a terrible word but my eyelids went on the flicker.

I think we both panicked for a moment as the lorry slewed around and nearly stopped but Pop recovered his wits and put his foot on the gas and we climbed over the last set of tracks to safety before we settled down. The motor died and a giant despair claimed me for its very own. Te Rotiha! The last place on God's earth! A flat five-fifty twenty-one at Te Rotiha!

As we climbed down from the cab there was a second explosion followed by a faint hiss which was plainly distinguishable from the hissing of the locomotive at the far end of the shunting yard. A sheep looked down at us from a bracken-covered embankment and munched steadily in a cynical sort of way. Pop leaned against the tray of the truck and hooked his thumbs in his pink underpants which showed over his trousers and for an awful minute I thought he was going to start howling.

"Neddy," he told me, "if ever a man wuz dogged by fate and hounded by circumstances beyond his control it's yuh ole dad Dee-aitch Poindexter. If there's another man walking the face of the globe who's seen as many blown out and punctured five-fifty twenty-ones as yours truly muh heart bleeds for him like a stuck pig. Words fail me when I think of the countless ignorant, no-hoper twots running around the countryside on six-hundred sixteens without a care in the world and not a man-jack among them that could tell a Shacklock stove from a worm-eaten dunny seat."

I could see the iron had entered Pop's soul in a big way this time. There was nothing I could say which would even begin to cheer him up so I leaned on the tray myself and hooked my thumbs in the top of my trousers. I never ever did find out where we were supposed to be going exactly, but there was a dirt road just ahead of us that wound up through the stock-yards to the top of the embankment and I suppose there was a load of junk up there somewhere that Pop or Uncle Athol had sniffed out.

We leaned there on the truck for a long time and never spoke a single word, just let the gloom of the place seep into our bones. I think I must have been nearly asleep when I heard Pop say, "Well, Jimmy Coleman! Fancy you coming across us like this. I'm a glad man to see yuh, Jim Coleman. If someone hadn't come along and spoken to a man soon in his current perdicment I don't know what I'd uh done."

Jim Coleman is my brother-in-law who had to get married to Constance. What a stroke of luck he was the guard on the train that was getting made-up down the line apiece. Wonders will never cease! And, of course, it was not long before he suggested we slip along and get into the guard's van and make home that way. It gladdened my heart to hear Jim Coleman come to light with that suggestion. Apart from being glad because it was a way of getting home, it was also going to be a new experience. I had never been on a train before.

"Looks like you'll hafta come back through the week, Pop," Jim Coleman said after he had pushed his cap back and scratched around in his skimpy, red hair. "If yuh kin raise a couple of tyres I'll see if I kin smuggle yuh back on the early goods some morning."

"Yuh'll never guess who's sitting out there in the carriage," Jim Coleman continued when we had scrambled up into the van. "There's a Mrs Breece and her niece and, stone the crows, if she isn't the aunt as well of this poor girl that's gone and got her throat cut. She's getting the kid away from it all for a while, she told me. You could've

22

knocked me down with a pick-axe when she told me she was this Daphne Moran's aunt."

"Yuh mean the girl that's been murdered down in the city?" I cried excitedly.

Before long the wheels beneath us began to move and gather speed.

So, buffeted by the wind and gingerly clutching for support the wheel I had been warned not to play with, I saw, through smoke-grimed glass, the niece of the murdered Daphne Moran and, also, long outstretched legs at the far end of the carriage.

I now know the legs belonged to the sinister man I had first glimpsed at the crossroads.

Much piecing together has been necessary — and not a little guesswork — to compile what follows. Let's face it — I have even made use of Uncle Athol for one part, but of course he didn't know he was helping. That man would have shut up like a clam if it had occurred to him he was being useful.

Chapter Three

A LARGE TRUCK, turning off the main highway into one of the narrow roads which shoot away and vanish like arrows aimed at the eternal haze of the backblocks, drew up at the crossroads a few hundred yards from the Te Rotiha railway station. When the truck rolled off on its way to the distant hills, it left a tall, gaunt man standing motionless beside the dusty road; for all the world, in the rays of the declining sun, like a scarecrow, strayed from the cloud-shadowed field. The shadow he cast heightened the impression of a scarecrow for, under his arm, he carried a cardboard box and this gave great width, in silhouette, to the shoulders of his flapping suit coat, as if his arms were spread. He topped the six-foot mark by three or four inches and was thin to the point of emaciation. He was hatless and balding. His suit, of some dark cloth, was old, crumpled, streaked with dust. The man looked derelict, like a person who has slept under a tree with a handkerchief over his face. That his grimy shirt was held together at the neck by a black bow tie was ridiculous, but some power emanating in and projected from the sunken eyes would have silenced derision. After some moments spent, apparently, in contemplation, he began to walk down the rough road to the smoke-blackened buildings in the hollow.

If a railway junction can also be a whistle stop then

24

Te Rotiha, twelve miles inland from Klynham, is both. Unless carrying passengers bound for Klynham or the coastal town of Oporenho, the express trains thunder contemptuously through Te Rotiha taking the curving track which hurtles towards the hills. There are only a pub and a grocery store to mark the existence of Te Rotiha to passing motorists, but the railway station is kept reasonably busy most of the time. There is always freight to and from the coast to be handled, and, to the station's own stock-yards, come daily consignments of cattle and sheep, dog-harried, lowing and bleating their way beneath umbrellas of dust along the lonely country roads. Even on this day, Sunday, the station displayed some signs of activity.

A youth wearing a peaked cap on the back of his head was seated behind the desk in the station office. He was day-dreaming and gave a violent start as a shadow fell across the desk. His mouth fell open at the sight of the freak-ugly face with its great jutting nose looming so near the top of the open doorway. In long, slow strides the gaunt stranger gathered his own shadow into an inky pool at his feet in front of the office desk.

The youth pointed out the ancient carriage standing on a back line to the lanky and mysterious-looking traveller who, without a word of thanks, stalked away and stepped down from the platform. He picked his way across the railway lines, the sound of the clinkers crushing beneath his feet ringing out clearly in this sleepy hollow.

"Now who the dickens is he?" muttered the youth. "Something weird about that rooster. Cop that bow tie. Another of ole McDermott's scrubcutters packed up and going off on a spree, I s'pose. They're all the same. Work out there in the sticks till they've got a wad that ud choke a bull and then wham—on the piss for a month. Whadda life."

Passengers who change trains at Te Rotiha for the coast

soon learn to hate the place. Mrs Breece and her twelve-year-old niece, Lynette, were fortunate that their introduction to Te Rotiha only involved a wait in the two-hour category and that it was passed in mild, early autumn sunshine. Even then, Lynette, normally a most patient and well-mannered child, began to fidget and find the delay interminable. Her supply of chocolate was exhausted. She had read all her comics again and again. The excitement of travelling had palled on her during the six-hour journey from the city and this long wait seemed to Lynette to be just about the last straw. She had been confined to her bed for some days with a fever and now she was tired and her head ached. Her aunt was no company for she fell asleep again almost as soon as Lynette managed to wake her, though how she managed to sleep propped up in a corner like that was beyond her young niece's understanding. Even when a wagon was shunted, with a resounding and shuddering crash, into the carriage they were trapped in, Mrs Breece only mumbled something and fell asleep again.

The carriage to which they had been directed to take their baggage and find seats was also the last straw in Lynette's opinion. After the crowded express with its deep, red leather seats, to be alone in this antediluvian carriage which featured narrow bench seats, as hard as those in a city tram, running the full length of each side, was a decided change for the worse. It impressed on Lynette just how far she was from home and to just what sort of Indian country she was being taken. On top of her other troubles she was already becoming homesick.

Every time the freight wagons crashed against the carriage, Lynette hoped that at last the train was made up and action was imminent, but soon she again heard the engine tooting at the far end of the yard, its puffing and hissing sounding maddeningly distant. At intervals a peaked cap passed along under the windows. The windows all refused to open. Lynette tried them all. She was frightened to leave her seat for long because whenever a wagon crashed into the carriage the jar was sufficiently violent to have sent her flying. A sheep regarded her from behind the wire fence on the top of the embankment behind the stock-yards. Lynette put her tongue out at the sheep. Having ascertained that her aunt was still asleep, she put her thumb against her snub nose and extended five fingers at the lugubrious animal. She made the same gesture at the top of the cap the next time it passed beneath her window.

Time went by and Lynette became so bored and angry that, when a door creaked open and they were joined by another passenger, she could have cheered. Although she had been reared in city streets which abounded in unusual-looking characters, her eyes became round as she studied the newcomer. He looked as tall as a lamp post and carried about the same amount of fat. His dishevelled dark suit of clothes hung limply around his bony structure. He was so thin, so gaunt, he looked as if he might belong to the walking dead. In spite of the censor's ruling, Lynette had recently seen not one, but an entire series of films about the walking dead and considered herself an authority on the subject.

"A zombie," she breathed. It was frightening, but it was an improvement on that sheep. She had moved too far along the seat to be able to nudge her aunt. The stranger's only luggage was a cardboard box which he placed on the seat. When he sat down himself he put one leg up on the opposite seat quite effortlessly. It was the longest and skinniest leg Lynette had ever seen. With claw-like hands he fumbled for a moment at the base of his scrawny neck and then rested the back of his balding head against the window. He looked very weary. Lynette now perceived he was wearing a black bow tie and still her wonder grew. However, to her deep disappointment the stranger showed the same infuriating capacity for sleep as her aunt. Within a moment or two she was caught in a cross-fire of snores from opposite ends of the compartment.

Even in sleep, however, the newcomer provided diversion. At intervals a shuddering groan escaped him. His legs twitched convulsively. It was obvious he was in the grip of a nightmare. Lynette who was a kind-hearted child felt that maybe she should awaken him. She knew what nightmares were like and was always glad when her father or mother woke her up. It seemed an awful cheek to wake up a perfect stranger, but a particularly harrowing groan convinced her that her duty was obvious. She arose and approached the ragged bundle of clothes and bones which heaved and sighed so unhappily.

At close range he looked more like a zombie than ever. His nose was enormous, like a beak. It was a nose roughly pitted all over and blue in colour. It says much for Lynette that she felt more sorry for its owner than nauseated. It also says much for her that she finally plucked up enough courage to reach out with the intention of shaking him by the shoulder.

With a bubbling cry the sleeper's mouth opened wide, revealing that he was entirely toothless and giving him the appearance, especially with the great curving nose above the mouth, of a dying eagle. The claw-like hands began to clutch at the air about him, as if to strangle the ghosts besetting his slumber. There was something horrible about those writhing fingers. Terrified, Lynette shrank back along the carriage.

Abruptly he awoke. His eyes jerked to where Lynette stood watching him, her hand pressed against her mouth.

"Hello," Lynette finally managed to quaver. She tried to smile.

He began to wipe the sweat from his face with the sleeve of his coat.

"You've had a nawful nightmare," Lynette decided to persevere.

28

The stranger dropped his arms across his knees and the lump in his throat above the bow tie flew up and down.

"At our house," said Lynette, "we always wake people up when we know they're having a nawful nightmare. It's having things like cheese for supper that give 'em to you, y'know. Have you been eating cheese?"

"And how did you know I've been having a nightmare mer love? Bin gabblin' away in mer sleep, I have no doubt."

The gummy cavern from which the hoarse voice emerged fascinated and repelled Lynette, but she felt pleased to have struck up a conversation at last even with an apparition such as this.

"No, but you sure have been moaning and groaning away to yourself something awful."

"Well then, it's time I took mer medersin. Mer doctor would be angry if he found I wasn't being a good boy and taking mer medersin at the recommended, appropriated intervals."

Lynette's laugh tinkled along the carriage. The man opened his cardboard box and produced a squat bottle.

"Don't you want a spoon?" Lynette asked, greatly concerned as the bottle was tilted at the patient's mouth. "My, but you're running a risk, not measuring it out."

"Long experience mer love—long experience. Man gets to know just what's the right dose, mer love."

"You must have a good doctor," observed Lynette, seating herself within a few feet of her strange companion, but on the opposite seat. "You look as if you're feeling better right away."

"I am, mer love."

Lynette watched the deep lines around the mouth in the gaunt face deepen into gullies. It occurred to her that he was smiling at her.

"Why do you wear that funny tie?" she asked; but at that moment the train jerked into motion and it was a

29

line of inquiry she neglected to pursue Twenty or so wagons ahead of the solitary passenger-coach with its three occupants, the engine bellowed angrily. The long train creaked and shuddered. Soon the bracken and fern-clad walls of the long cutting just out of Te Rotiha dwindled to barbed-wire fences. Across rolling farmland, with its homesteads and haystacks and shelter belts of pine and macrocarpa the train, ironically referred to as the 4.30, lumbered coastward. The countryside was already becoming gloomy.

Searching her mind for some conversational gambit to keep her intriguing fellow traveller from falling asleep again (his chin was slumped down on his chest) Lynette hit upon an idea. Steadying herself against the edge of the long seat, she made her way down the length of carriage to the corner where her aunt slept. From her aunt's knitting basket she abstracted a rolled-up copy of a city newspaper's morning edition. She had amused herself earlier on, by reading the headlines upside down and back to front, but her aunt had refused to hand her the paper.

"It's horrible, Lynette," she had said. "It's not fit to be read by little girls who've been sick. Read your comics, dear, and think of the nice holiday by the sea we're going to have. The last time you went to Oporenho you weren't knee high to a grasshopper, and you've forgotten what it's like to have the beach at your back door-step."

Place of honour on the front page of the paper had been allotted to a photograph of a smiling Daphne Moran, Lynette's own second cousin. Beneath black, arresting headlines summarizing the progress made in the search for the slayer, ran the second-day story of the young theatre usherette who had vanished and whose ravished, nude body had been discovered the following day by boys sailing boats on a pond. The body had been semi-submerged in a weed-choked corner of the pond. Daphne Moran's throat had been cut.

Despite their relationship, Lynette had hardly known Daphne Moran at all. Her childish mind was scarcely able fully to grasp the stark horror of what had occurred and her excitement at being even remotely associated with such a sensational event far outweighed any feeling of grief. That her relationship to the murdered girl made her a mighty important person was a suspicion that Lynette had had confirmed by the veiled conversation between her aunt and the guard earlier on in the journey. It had been veiled but it had not fooled Lynette one little bit. The guard's eyes had nearly popped out of his head when he had found out who they were. First the illness which had confined her to the sick-room and now this trip to the seaside had outwitted Lynette's hopes of cashing-in on her reflected notoriety; but seeing her chance now, she took it.

The guard saved her the chore of actually re-awakening the tall, scarecrow-like man in the corner. When the door of the carriage opened to admit the guard, the sudden cyclone of black smoke and cold air and roar of the wheels which entered along with him awakened even her aunt.

Lynette had known for some time that the guard had been standing on the platform of their carriage. She had been just able to discern his shape through the soot-grimed glass panels of the door. She had carefully opened up her newspaper and then folded it again, so that she could thrust the picture of Daphne Moran under the man's very eyes. Now she dropped the paper on the seat beside him and stumbled back to her aunt's end of the coach.

"Sit down, Lynette," said her aunt. "Heavens, girl, don't run all over the place the moment I doze off."

The guard lit one of the dome-shaped oil lamps in the roof and then stood over the huddled figure of the strange man who fumbled for money to purchase his ticket. Then he descended swayingly on Lynette and her aunt, pausing on the way to open the glass and ignite the wicks of two more lamps.

"Next stop, Klynham," he informed them. "You'll be into Oporenho in time for tea."

The guard, having punched their tickets, returned to his van immediately aft of the passenger coach. The door slammed on the racket of the wheels. Miles ahead, it seemed, the engine hooted.

Now Lynette's mouth fell open in astonishment. At the other end of the carriage the man who suffered from nightmares was on his feet, arms above his head as if in abject terror. He was grey-faced, gibbering. He shrank back against the door.

"Aunty, aunty," said Lynette, urgently. "Look, look!"

"What is it?" said her aunt. "This must be Klynham."

Lynette looked out and saw the scattered lights of a town in the gathering dusk. When she looked along the carriage again there was only the folded newspaper on the seat to be seen. The cardboard box had dematerialized and so had her favourite zombie. For a man who looked so old and ill he must have whirled about and ducked away at incredible speed. Either that or the encounter had been all a dream. Lynette opened her mouth to address her aunt but sighed and closed it again. She had a feeling it would be just a waste of breath to tell her aunt about the zombie man.

The train gradually creaked to a standstill. Things banged and a voice shouted. Lynette rubbed a hole in the mist on the closest window and pressed her snub nose against the cold glass. She thought she glimpsed a shadow, like that of a huge bird, stumbling across the tracks into the gloom.

When Pop and I had jumped down from the guard's van at Klynham and sneaked back along the line a little way as we knew Jim Coleman wanted us to do, Pop said,

"I'll go over and see Connie for awhile. Yuh just tell yuh mother I'll be back home shortly and if yuh take my advice yuh'll steer clear of elaborating on our disastrous journey as if ever there was a woman to make a mountain out of a molehill and vicky verky it's yuh good mother, bless her heart."

And so I found myself following the sinister scarecrow man up the dusky streets. It makes my flesh creep to remember.

Chapter Four

Aᴛʜᴏᴜɢʜ ᴛʜᴇʀᴇ had been no steady rain, no downpour, for over a week, there was a big puddle of water in the middle of Klynham's main street. It was always there, even in the heart of summer. It was a feature of the town. It had nothing to do with rain, but owed its existence to subterranean forces, seepage, impermeable strata and so on. The puddle was right outside the Federal Hotel and had been the looking-glass of many dissolute visages, many coyly lopsided moons. One night when the wide street was empty and the moon shepherded a few dark clouds from well aloft the puddle gave to an evil face a setting of jewels and muddy mountains. The face was owned by a phenomenally tall man and the devil himself could not have conspired with a street lamp to cast a longer shadow. It was also the face of a phenomenally thirsty man. A tongue flicked parched lips, eyes sought in vain for a chink of light, some flaw in the armour of the Federal Hotel. He began to cross the road. The puddle, automatically skirted, faithfully recorded his stealthy, purposeful passing.

Ever since, earlier that night, he had jumped down from the coast-bound train, Hubert Salter, for such was the tall man's name, had been skulking in a back street, concealing himself in the shadows of Hardley & Manning's rear entrance. No one had gone past. He had crouched back against the door when he had seen a group of figures gather on the corner, but it was only the Salvation Army band, who almost immediately began to serenade the deserted streets. To the sound of hymns and, in the intervals, the preacher's upbraiding and vehement voice, Salter finished off his squat bottle of schnapps. The alcohol dispersed his fears. He began to feel certain that he had been in panic-stricken flight from nothing more tangible than his over-wrought imagination. He cursed his folly. He was glad he had slipped away from the city, given such a golden chance, although there would have been little danger in remaining; but to end up in a little township like this, in the still of a Sunday evening was dangerously conspicuous. At Oporenho, small as it was, there would have been the port and the big freezing-works with its army of seasonal workers to absorb him. Even in the remote event of being questioned Salter could have proved that, always in the past, whenever the current travelling show he had been with had folded, he had headed for a port and freezing-works town to seek casual employment.

"The wolf bane is blooming again," Salter muttered. The highlight of his life over the last few days suddenly flashed back to numb his brain. Ecstasy flooded his loins and his genitals.

"And say unto you, I am Jesus," came the preacher's voice. The drum began to thump and the band struck up again.

"Yes, and I am Death," proclaimed Salter dramatically, peering crazily up from his hiding place at the moon which was drifting at a cock-eyed angle over the Jubilee Hotel. He began to mutter crazily to himself, and hammered against his temples with his fists. Crouching down he sought through his cardboard box for the butt of a cigarette. The box contained a strange assortment: coloured handkerchiefs, billiard balls, a black velvet bag, a length of silken cord, a wand and so on. There was even a pair of handcuffs. The half-smoked cigarette was in an

35

unusual type of tumbler that featured a mirror partition. When Salter lit the cigarette the acrid smell of hashish filled his nostrils. Eagerly and deeply he inhaled, holding the smoke in his lungs for as long at a time as he was able.

Raising his head he saw out of the corner of an eye the reflection of his great beak of a nose in the glass doorway of the shop. A cry escaped him. The reflection went back and back along the tunnel of the years. The sequinned pink tights and big beautiful legs of Zita, his assistant in the great mind-reading act, loomed up in the reflection. One of her hands rested on the arm of a wavy-headed young man and her pretty face was twisted in a sneer. They did not know that Salter, in the mirror, had seen them sneering at him, sneering at Salter the Sensational. For a long time he had roamed the benighted amusement park and then he had seen her shadow against the lamplight in her tent, as she wriggled her plump, soft buttocks to discard what little she did wear. Exultantly the crimson haze had befogged his brain. That night fire had raged through the camp and destroyed for ever her ravished, sneering body. So easy it had been. So almost unbelievably exciting. Such mad exhilaration, such sexual power the mad, evil moment granted. So easy it must always be.

The reefer was scorching Salter's lips. The Salvation Army band was packing up. Salter chuckled. Coming from the dark doorway, the chuckle had a devilish sound.

As soon as Alf Yerbey, the licensee of the Federal Hotel, heard the rap on the back door he switched off the light in the little back bar. The only illumination now came from the passage, through a transom. Alf Yerbey's main reason for switching off the light was to impress on his customers the importance of keeping silent. He knew the futility of trying to shush men who had been drinking beer for some hours; but he knew, by switching off the light, he could temporarily shut up even the most garrulous and intoxicated of his Sunday night customers.

In the dim light the men slid coins and cigarettes off the bar and returned them to their pockets. They began to shuffle into an adjoining room, a store-room that had bottles of beer and wine in crates and cartons stacked half-way up three of its walls. Only a stranger, or the police, would have rapped on the back door in such a way. Anybody who was in the know would have scratched on the door three times with a coin.

In the gloom the publican lifted the flap in the bar and stepped through it. Besides himself, the only person who had not evacuated the bar was Charlie Dabney, the undertaker, who was perched up on a stool peering owlishly around.

"Great Scott," mumbled Charlie Dabney. "The jondomorohso. The minions of the law, what, what. Ignorant pack of bastards. No respect for gracious living. Place cordoned off. Innocent citizens—"

"Ssssh, sssh," said Alf Yerbey.

"Victimized," concluded the plump little undertaker, clamping the corner of his mouth tightly on an unlit cigar which waggled uncertainly. He nodded solemnly and then looked up abruptly. "Nicely put?"

"Very nicely put, Charlie," said Alf Yerbey, who had no intention of offending his most regular customer and biggest spender by far.

"Why can't they go catch a burglar or something?" Charlie demanded to be told. "People getting murdered right left 'n' centre. Hotbed crime. Gutters running red with gore. Assassins looking every friggin' doorway. Wharah police do? Cordon off friggin' pub. Storm last bastion of gracious living. Nicely put?"

"Certainly Charlie," said Alf Yerbey.

"Wheresh Athol?" said Charlie Dabney. "Need moral support in this, our darkest hour."

Hearing the mention of his name, Athol Cudby peered out of the store-room.

"You're all right, Claude," said the publican. "Charlie's booked into room twenty-three as usual and you can be his guest. Keep your money out of sight while I see who the hell it is. Let me do the talking."

When he said "room twenty-three" he spoke louder and looked hard at Charlie Dabney, who was never able to remember his room number when he was questioned by the police. Although Charlie Dabney's place of business, which also served him for a home, was just across the alley from the hotel, the police had finally recognized that they would never convict him for after-hour drinking, unless they caught him in the White Hart or Commercial. He had a permanent room (which he never occupied) and sat down to quite a number of meals (without eating anything) at the Federal. Charlie Dabney was a well known oddity in the town. Some called him "old Nicely Put" others "old Episode Closed". Everyone agreed he was a "dag", a "real dag". He had been mixed up in some extraordinary and side-splitting incidents. The last of the Dabneys, he appeared to have almost completely ruined the business and yet still have a supply of folding money as limitless as the twinkle in his eye. Everyone liked him, except for a few wives who had waited all night in vain for the return of their spouses, but he was a man to be avoided like the plague, unless one had a few days to spare. To be lured into his shop for a convivial spot was disastrous. The place was stocked with enough food and booze (all hidden in the queerest places) to withstand a siege.

The knock came again. Whoever it was had, by this time, rapped on the back door several times.

When Alf Yerbey opened the door his heart sank. The height of the shadowy figure standing at the foot of the steps suggested officialdom.

"What is it?" he asked. "Whadda yuh want?"

"Mer friend," said the tall stranger. "Please forgive me influctuating on yer at this hour uv night. I am a stranger in yer town, stranded here on account of a breakdown in mer limousine."

He laughed hoarsely and laid a hand on the publican's elbow. The light from the passage now illuminated his gaunt countenance. Alf Yerbey's fear of a raid was completely set at rest by the colour of the stranger's nose. He had not been a hotel-keeper twenty years for nothing. He was puzzled and intrigued by the black bow tie.

"If yer would be so kind," said Salter, "as to provide me with some refreshment, preferably of an alcoholic and reviving natchuh. Quite candidly, sir, I feel that, unless I have a drink, there is some doubt of me surviving the night. I spent yesterday, sir, with a hectic school of frothblowers and all day I have been travelling and suffering the agonies of hell. If the milk of human kindness flows in yer veins, yer will not turn me from yer hospitable door."

Salter also was no novice at appraising his man. In Alf Yerbey's veined and blotched countenance and distended abdomen, he had recognized the gateway to sympathy.

When the light clicked on in the bar the men who had been skulking in the store-room emerged and inspected Salter slyly and curiously.

"Yer will join me, sir?" asked Salter when he had put the cardboard box he was carrying down at his feet and been given a double schnapps. The publican declined. Salter drank three doubles in as many minutes. He then purchased a packet of cigarettes. It was to be observed that his hands were shaking. Salter's hands, after the first shock of his overall appearance had been digested, were always the next feature to attract attention. They were hands that would have been noticeably large on a bushwhacker and yet they were as sensitive-looking and as cared-for as those of a concert pianist. He offered a cigarette to Athol Cudby who was standing alongside him.

"Thank yuh kindly," said Athol Cudby, taking the

cigarette and holding up a crooked finger of his free hand in unctuous acknowledgment.

"My name is Cudby," he said. "Athol Cudby."

"Salter, Hubert Salter."

"My friend Mr Charles Dabney—Mr Salter."

"Deelighted to make yer acquaintance."

"Deelighted also. Also delighted not policeman. Horror of policeman. Positively allergic policemen any shape or form. Only hanging on in business for pleasure of burying policeman some day. Bound to come one day. Ole Charlie'll have the last laugh, never fear."

"Mr Dabney is our local mortician," explained Athol Cudby in his soft-voiced fashion.

"Well now," said Salter. "That's a very interesting profession, I'm sure, sir. And lucrative I imagine." He laughed hoarsely. "All flesh is as grass, sir."

"People just dying to meet ole Charlie," said the little undertaker, his unlit and well-chewed cigar waggling up and down all the time he spoke. "See 'em all go down the main street yet. But shed many a tear. But not when police kick the bucket. If a man was having a cup of coffee, who'd be the first bastard to come along and test it with a hydrometer? Smith! Great Scott, Mr Salter, you won't credit the depth a man could stoop to till you've lived in this town under Smith."

"Smith is our sergeant," explained Athol Cudby. "A very bad man is Sergeant Smith. No love lost between him and Charlie."

"Pig of a man," said the undertaker. "Never understand gracious living. Not as long as his hole points at the ground. Watch a pub all night, leaning up against a bank doorway while burglars taking the safe out the back way. See a man lying in the gutter with a knife sticking out of his back and he'd arrest him for being inebriated."

The cigar waggled furiously and Charlie Dabney's chest and shoulders heaved with mirth. Athol Cudby sniggered.

The gullies of flesh in the tall stranger's jowls deepened. He was smiling, but his thoughts were on the rapidly diminishing pile of change beside his glass on the counter. A financial crisis was one double schnapps distant. If he had managed to reach Oporenho that night he would have soon sniffed out a card game among the freezing-workers, but this town presented a very different picture. In Oporenho he would have kept the uncanny skill of his fingers a close secret but here, he reflected, it might be more profitable to openly startle the natives with some sleight of hand.

"Yuh right enough," said Alf Yerbey as he refilled the glasses. He addressed the stranger. "Our sergeant here gives the pubs hell. Examines our registers every damn' night that passes without fail. Offends bono feedo guests drinking in the lounge. Positively sits on a man's friggin' doorstep. Do you know what the bastard did once?"

Salter shook his head.

"Swang on a man's legs to break his neck," said Alf Yerbey.

" 'S'fact," said Athol Cudby. "True as a man stands here tonight."

"When this Smith was pounding a beat," explained Yerbey, "he was at a hanging at Mount Davidson. They dropped a guy through the hatch and they made a balls of it. Smith was the guy who grabbed hold of his ankles and swung his sixteen stone on him to snap his neck like a rotten parsnip."

Alf Yerbey found the reaction to this macabre tit-bit extremely gratifying. He had related it times without number and was always sure of seeing horror register on the faces of his audience, but the tall man seemed positively overwhelmed. His face went chalk-white and he grabbed at the edge of the bar.

"Gives yuh some idea, eh?" Alf Yerbey chuckled, taking the man's glass away to replenish it.

" 'S'fact," said Athol Cudby " 'S'solid fact. True as a man stands here tonight in this very room."

"Drink's on me," said Charlie Dabney. He fumbled with his wallet, watched anxiously by three eyes and one cunningly constructed of glass. Athol Cudby retrieved the wallet when it fell to the floor.

"Drinks on me. Inshish, inshish," proclaimed the little old mortician. He momentarily stayed the waggling of his cigar when Salter leaned across and held a match to its end.

"Allow me," said Salter. The hand holding the match was shaking badly. .

Several more rounds of drinks were served and consumed and still the small heap of silver in front of the stranger remained intact. Athol Cudby, quick to recognize opportunism in a rival, studied the newcomer covertly with a beady and suspicious eye. His fingers, when they were not occupied with either a glass or a cigarette, fidgeted in the lining of his trouser pockets. In his sulky preoccupation he failed to hear the blandishments which prevailed on Charlie Dabney to suddenly hand over his big gold watch to the stranger. Athol Cudby started violently.

Salter took up a position half-way around the oval bar, from whence he was clearly visible to all present.

"Gentlemen," he said. His tone of voice, his great height, the bow tie, contributed to a presence which commanded and was granted a sudden silence. The murmur of several voices tailed off resentfully.

"I have 'ere in mer hand," said Salter, holding up by its chain the outsize gold watch, "the timepiece of our good friend and well-known citizen, Mister Charles Dabney. None of us have the slightest doubt but that it is a very valuable gen-u-ine gold watch of great antiquity and reliability. In addition to its value as a gen-u-ine gold

42

timepiece, I am also informed by its owner that its senti-
mental value is incalculating."

Salter laid the watch on the bar in full view of everybody and stepped back. He pushed back his sleeves and
tucked them under to keep them there. He held his hands
aloft, fixing the watch with a glittering gaze. His wrists,
bared and curving, were like necks of geese.

"Great Scott," said Charlie Dabney, enjoying himself
immensely.

Salter now produced a large handkerchief and, holding
it by the top corner, displayed to all that it was innocently
empty back and front. He gave the handkerchief to a man
standing nearby. The man examined it gingerly at first
but, reassured by its cleanliness, thoroughly enough. Salter
emitted a throaty chuckle. He dropped the handkerchief
over the gold watch on the bar.

"Yer will observe," he said, spreading the handkerchief
out with one or two gossamer flicks of his long fingers,
"that this most valuable timepiece is still visible through
the thin material. If anyone present entertains the slightest doubt they are at liberty to investigate."

No one moved. Everyone was watching intently. Salter
stooped down and removed one of his shoes. "This little
illusion, which I bring you tonight," he announced, "is
known as 'The passing of time', or, in certain circles in
the *mistykeist*, 'The crack of dawn'."

Salter brought the heel of his shoe down with a splintering crack on top of the handkerchief. He raised his hand
again, but Athol Cudby leaped forward and caught his
upraised arm. Salter fixed him with his weirdly compelling
gaze. Athol Cudby fell back.

"Great Scott," mumbled Charlie Dabney.

The heel of the shoe fell savagely several times. No one
had any doubt by now that the stranger in their midst was
as mad as an elephant with earache. But nobody moved.
The tall lunatic gathered up the debris of the watch in the

43

handkerchief and held it aloft like a miniature plum pudding in its cloth.

"I see by all yer faces," he said, "that the ruthless destruction of this valuable timepiece of incalculating value has not left a single one of yer unmoved. By the powers of magic vested in me, I will now endeavour to undo the damage I have done. Only endeavour, mark my words. I can make no promises. Only if the gods of darkness and magic are favourable, can I restore Mr Dabney his precious gen-u-ine gold timepiece."

A low moan escaped the owner of the watch. Salter began a mumbled incantation and then shook out the handkerchief. A gasp greeted the fact that it was empty. Salter dropped the handkerchief and flashed his weird eyes around the bar. He approached Athol Cudby and lifted, from that horrified gentleman's head, his battered slouch hat. He groped in the hat and withdrew from it, held delicately by the chain, the late-lamented gold watch.

"Great Scott," exclaimed Charlie Dabney in vast relief. "A magician. A jolly ole wizard. The lights won't go out all night."

Salter, having modestly consumed the double schnapps with which his skill was rewarded, now proceeded to hoax and amuse the patrons of the Federal Hotel back bar for some time. At last he declined to perform further on the ground of excessive weariness. He became involved in a deep conversation with Charlie Dabney.

"Great Scott," the undertaker exclaimed from time to time. "Sensational, magnificent. We'll amalgamate, sir. With your skill and my coffins we'll rock this town to its foundations. We go together like Gilbert and Sullivan. We gravitate to each other like a boiled carrot to a hunk of corn brisket. Nicely put?"

"Very nicely—" began Athol Cudby.

The undertaker struck the bar in great excitement. "This is what I've been waiting for. Athol here knows I'm investing in one of those neon signs. Off and on all night. Too many of the old families in these parts going past ole Charlie lately. Have a wagon sent up from one of those upstart undertakers to take ole Dad's body all the way to the crematorium at Highriver would they? It's degrading. Fellows are a disgrace to the profession. Not even got a decent hearse with flowers painted on it. It's high time people around here were made to realize it's just as important to die in a dignified way as it is to live graciously. You're the answer to my prayer, Mr Salter."

The tall man rubbed his hands together gleefully.

"Yer may count on me, sir," he chuckled.

"Neon sign going off and on all night. *The dignity of death. The dignity of death.* How does that sound, eh, eh—"

"*Cremations arranged,*" put in Athol Cudby. "I thought that was what it was gunna be. I like that better."

The cigar ceased to waggle as the undertaker digested Athol Cudby's interjections.

"*Cremations—*" began Athol Cudby, but Charlie Dabney held up a stern hand to silence him. He spent a few moments in rapt cogitation and then slapped the bar triumphantly.

"Great Scott! A revelation! I've got it! See it clear as the tadpoles in that water carafe. Heh, heh. Episode closed. Can't you see their faces! Can't you see their mouths hanging open like the addled-brained nincompoops they are, when they see that sign flicking on and off all night! And dear ole frien' here, Mr Salter, in the window sawing through a coffin with some young popsie in a nightdress inside it. It'll create a furore. Dabney and Son, the ole firm. Great Scott, we'll put these upstarts over at Highriver clean outa business."

Chapter Five

Monday, tongue in cheek, dawned bright and clear. Les Wilson walked half-way home with me in the dinner hour and we were the happiest. Victor Lynch had not even looked in our direction at school and his lieutenant, Skin Hughson, had actually nodded at Les, so Les informed me.

I ran along our dirt path, saw a tall man standing on the veranda, without taking much notice. Then I saw his helmet, missed the top step and hit the deck flat on my face. The cop gave me a hand up. Ma was in the kitchen wringing her hands. Out came Uncle Athol, shaky and bloodshot-eyed, with a pink singlet done up around his neck and showing above his grey shirt. He was as unshaven as an albino hedgehog, but he had his teeth in.

"C'mon, Cudby," said the cop. "Oi know, Oi know. It's all a terrible mistake, but we'll straighten everything out down at the sta-hayshun."

I went into my bedroom. I could not tell if I was shaking with fear or relief.

Herbert was still in bed, which was not actually a new development. We watched the cop and Uncle Athol get into a big sedan car (in which, I little dreamed, I was to have one of the most hair-raising rides of my life) and drive off. Herbert lit a cigarette with a shaking hand.

"What a start for the day," he said. "Cripes, that give

46

me a turn. That's undone all the good of a night's rest, that has. What's the old tit done?"

"Dunno." I went to take one of Herbert's cigarettes, but he grabbed the packet.

"Thought yuh wanted to be a six-footer."

"I've changed muh mind, I'm gunna be a jockey." I made a grab for the smokes, but just then Ma came in carrying on something awful.

"What a disgrace!" she cried. "There's Athol dragged off in handcuffs to the cop-shop and yuh father as drunk as a coot on a Monday. This is the end of us around this burg. I might as well give up the ghost right now. Many's the time I've said there's trouble just around the corner and now it's all coming true on a bloody Monday. Yuh father'll be picked up for being drunk-in-charge as sure as eggs're eggs and that'll be the stone end of the whole caboosh. If Grandma uz here, she'd drop down stone dead from shame, and so would I. What a beginning for the week with a tub full of washing. Poor little Eddy, get yourself some bread and jam, yuh poor little boy. Yuh mother's nearly all in and can't bring her mind around to thinking of food. I've had a terrible shock seeing that cop standing there on the door-step, and yuh father as drunk as a coot."

Pop was standing with his back to the stove, the nape of his neck against the mantelpiece and his hands behind his back. I had noticed the Dennis in the yard so there had obviously been a rescue expedition to Te Rotiha. By Pop's appearance, the operation had not been all work and no play. I could tell by the way his head was wagging from side to side, he was a real job all right. I had to work in behind him to see if there was any stew in the pot. There was a spoonful of stew with a carrot in it.

"Ducashun," said Pop. "Sathing. Ducashun. Be lawyuh, doctuh. Go school, get ducashun. Breeding gets yuh nowhere. Gotta have lottsa dough and ducashun. Police got no breeding. Got no friggin' ducashun either. Poor ole Athol. Whitesh man Chris' ever put breath into. Gunna miss ole Athol. Get legal counsel. Bes' money can buy. Kayshee if neshry. Money no object. Disgrace firm Daitch Poindexter Gross miscarriage jusch."

I got some bread and butter and sat up at the end of the table with my spoonful of stew.

"Fowls," said Pop. "Hic."

That was one spoonful of stew that bore a charmed life. I put it back on the plate.

"Fowls," Pop went on. "Ole Athol wouldn't stoop to stealing fowls. Can't stoop anyway. Got a rupchuh."

He started chortling idiotically.

"Couldn't pull a friggin' fowl off the nest," he gurgled.

I heard Prudence coming in and pounded out to head her off. Dolly and Monica were right on her heels, so I beckoned her into the washhouse.

"Crummy," she said, when I told her the goings on. I paced up and down the washhouse like a nut. Prudence came back.

"It's fowls, awright," she said. "That's what the police have got him over. He's been raffling fowls all over town every Saturday and they reckon he's been stealing 'em. Ma said it was Lynch's fowls that got pinched. Whatcha gunna do, Ned?"

I sat down on the W.C. seat. As far as I was concerned this was the end of the trail.

"Whatcha gunna do?" Prudence worried. "He never took any fowls. You did. Maybe he's got an alleyway."

I said nothing. What could I say? Prudence said, "Well I gotta have something to eat. I didn't have any brekker this morning."

I high-tailed it down to Wilson's and now it was my turn to spoil someone's dinner. I will grant Les this, he made the only sensible suggestion to date.

"Well, one thing's fuh sure," he said. "We can't go to

school. We gotta go somewhere quiet where we can use our brains."

The thought of locking ourselves in Fitzherbert's shed with all that gang of poultry was too much, so we headed for the dam. We stretched out under a pine-tree, which grew out over the water. The pine sadly contemplated its image, impaled on the reeds, while we tried to marshal our wits.

"The trouble is," Les kept pointing out, "we haven't got enough grata. We don't know what to do because we don't know what's going on. The old boy might have wriggled out of it. We'll just have to have more grata."

"I'll just have to confess, if he hasn't," I said. "I'm not a complete ratbag."

"Neither am I," said Les hotly. "I'll confess too. But I'll tell you something, Ned Poindexter, and that is I know who is a ratbag."

"Who?"

"Yeruncle Athol," he said. After a while he said, "How d'yuh know it wasn't our chooks he stole? How d'yuh know it wasn't yuh preshus Uncle Athol who took our Black Orphingtons and not Victor Lynch at *tall*?"

We gaped at each other.

"It adds up," said Les excitedly. "These fowls he was raffling. That musta been on Saturday. Pru told yuh it was Saturday. The raid on our coop was Friday night. Doesn't that ring a bell?"

"By cripes, but we did the Lynch job on Saturday night. How do the police tie that up with Uncle Athol raffling 'em on Saturday in the daytime? Howja count fuh that?"

"P'raps he's been at it all along. P'raps he's been flogging chooks right and left for a long time. This job of ours mighta just been the last straw."

"But Les, he helped us build that coop. Surely he wouldn't be such an absolute barstid?"

"According to my father," Les said firmly, "he's the biggest barstid yud meet in a day's march. According to my father, if Mr Cudby was around and yuh had any gold in yuh teeth, yud be running an awful risk going to sleep with yuh mouth open. According—"

I winced. "Don't keep on saying 'according to my father'," I rasped. "I heard yuh the first time. Awright then, so Uncle Athol is a ratbag, but the point is he's in the boob for stealing chooks and for all we know it might be the same chooks we took from Lynch's. Pru said it was Lynch's chooks the stink was over. We gotta find out where we stand. We gotta know what's happening."

"Well, didn't I say that?" said Les. "We gotta have more grata. That's what I said before. Unless we get some more grata we just can't figure anything out at*tall*. We just don't know what course of action to 'dopt. Not without grata, Ned."

It seemed no time at all before we heard the school bell in the distance.

"Time sure goes a lot quicker playing the wag than it does at school," Les observed gloomily. "Almost wish we'd gone now. Now we'll be in the cart at school on top of everything. It's not as if we've been able to figure anything out. We just haven't got the grata to think anything out. Now if only we could see a young lady, in the nood, with her throat cut, floating on that pond, like those jokers in the city did, we'd really give the cops something to think about."

"Yeah," I said absently. "WHAT!"

"Well, wouldn't we? That ud stop all this fuss about a few chooks. And if they blamed yeruncle Athol for it, it wouldn't be any of our dern business."

"That's a terrible business, Les. I told you I saw her aunt and cousin on the train, didn't I? And they haven't caught anybody yet. Ask me, all the cops are good for is hounding down poor devils like Uncle Athol and me'n you. I wonder who it was?"

"Now how in hell should I know! Thas one thing you can say about living in a sleepy hole like Klynham—yuh don't meet real bad sods like that. I wonder what those kids felt like when they saw her floating on the pond with her throat cut from ear to ear? Water red as red ink like as not. Can't yuh just imagine what that poor sheila musta looked like, Neddy, floating there with her throat gaping open from ear to ear, in the nood, and the water red as ink all around. Can'tcha just see the sorta bubbles—"

"Now look here, Les," I said, having had just about enough of this, "the way you're going on you'd think *we had* found her. I've just about had a gutzfull uv the way you go on and on about things. Honestly yud think nothing would please yuh more than if yuh did find a nood sheila with her throat cut from—floating on the lake."

"In the nood," said Les. "According to my father he's a necro something or other."

"Who is?"

"The guy that cut this poor sheila's throat from ear to ear. According to my father—I listened to what he was saying outside the door—he's a guy that has inter something with sheilas when they're conked. According to my father the police have found out that this guy conks them first and then roots them and that makes him the saddest guy and a necro something."

"Now is that so? Well, Les, you certainly surprise me. I'm not quite sure I quite understand this conks and then roots them business."

"Well neither am I, Neddy," Les confessed. "But you can take it from me thas the general idea. It's what my father said to my mother and he wouldn't be kidding *her*."

"Well it makes me sick."

Les made no answer and after a while I looked over at him. He was stretched out with one arm and one leg held stiffly up in the air, and he had the screwiest look on his face as if he had thrown a fit. It gave me a nasty start.

"Les," I said uneasily, "Whatta hell. Snap out uv it."

"I'm conked," he informed me out of the corner of his mouth. "Root me."

"I'll root you awright," I hissed, pouncing on him, "and I'll cut yuh throat and chuck yuh in the lake too, you see if I don't."

Some days I could beat Les and some days he could beat me and some days nobody won. In the end we would just collapse. This was one of those collapsing days. After the battle royal we made our way back to town and bid each other an exhausted "Abyssinia" at the corner—just a couple of good pals, with muddy knees, sweaty spines and a toss-up who had the most pine-needles down his shirt.

The very youthful policeman, who came to our place on Monday night with a portable typewriter, was called Ramsbottom. I am not going to divulge what we called him. No amount of kidding around, "Oh go on, do tell," will prevail. It is just too vulgar altogether.

The whole business was highly irregular, as I can see. The police wanted us to go to the station, but Ma had apparently gone into a flat spin and it does not surprise me in the least, knowing how Ma can go when she gets into overdrive, that the cops threw in the sponge.

When the cop arrived he asked for a side room to take our statements in, one by one, and Ma went into another nose-dive. Our kitchen did not have much decor to speak of, but alongside the other rooms it was a Louis Quinze salon. The young constable solved this brightly by suggesting that he took over this room and we all waited in the passage, or somewhere, but this was as far as he got.

"What and freeze!" said Ma, although it was such a balmy night we had let the stove go out. "Freeze us up to a state where we'd say the first thing that popped into our head I s'pose. Oh no, yuh don't, and have yuh putting words into muh children's mouth to swear away their innocence. I've heard all about those tricks, thank yuh very much, and it doesn't suit me at all to letcher get away with it under muh very nose. The truth will prevail, by Jesus, and it's my avowed intention and Mr Poindexter's too, to see that the innocent are not going to suffer while we freeze to a state where we say the first thing that pops into our head."

"I feel shuah," began Pop, who was only just feeling his way, having spent the afternoon in the sack.

"Mr Poindexter feels sure and so does Mr Cudby," Ma went on, "that the interests of justice will be best served by us all remaining in here together in this room, having a council of war, and everyone saying his piece until the whole shameful business is brought to a satisfactory collusion. My husband and me feel badly mortified to have the arm of the law under our very roof on account of the drunken foolishness of muh brother. In spite of all his drunken foolishness and the trouble it has brought into our dwelling on a Monday I feel it is only Christian to remember that Athol has never been the same since he lost his eye and been rupchud."

"Natalie," said Uncle Athol, feebly, "I feel sure—"

"You go to hell!" said Ma. "Yuv brought enough trouble and disaster to our very door-step. Now, officer, let's get on with this here intergration and third degree."

So that was that. The only victory to the law was that Herbert, who tried to sidle nonchalantly into the night, was brought back and allotted a chair next to Uncle Athol. Even then it was not long (the instant his statement had been taken) before Herbert managed to dematerialize.

"Moi noime," Constable Ramsbottom recited, reading my own statement back to me that night, "is Edward Clifton Poindexter and Oi reside with moi pah-harents at their residence Number one 'undred and foive, Winchester Street. Moi age is fourteen and Oi am a pupil attending Klynham Primary School."

Under the unshaded electric light bulb a bottle or so of haircream glistened on the cop's wavy, dark hair.

"On the noight uv the ther-rud 'aving completed moi 'omework . . ." He paused craftily. " 'Istory did you say?"

"Jography," I said promptly. No flies on me.

"That's right, jography," he mused, crestfallen. "Oi returned to moi bedroom which I share with moi older brother, 'Erbert. From 'ere it drifted to moi ears—is that what you said?"

"It drifted to my ears," I said, sticking to my guns.

"It drifted to moi ears the sound of Uncle Athol snoring. 'E was obviously sound asleep. This would have been approximately eight p.m. till ten p.m. After this Oi moi-self—"

I felt myself tensing. Constable Ramsbottom gave me a hard look. The haircream started investigating his forehead.

"Was claimed by the arms and legs of Morphia," I said firmly. I'd read that in a book and no lowbrow was going to talk me out of it.

"Was claimed by the arms and legs of Morphia. 'Ow do you spell that, young feller?"

I smiled in a rather superior way. "M-o-r-f-e-a-r, of course."

Constable Ramsbottom peered dubiously at the statement. He resumed. "On the previous Saturday morning Oi 'ad purchased from the Klynham Traders six Black Orphington fowls. Oi did this in company with Les Wilson of Camden Street, who goes to school with me. He went halves with me and we were the joint owners of the aforementioned Black Orphingtons. On the morning uv the ther-rud we discovered these fowls to be missing from

54

their coop, situated in the yard behind my pah-harents' residence. We were aware that a theft had taken place, but made no complaint."

I dared not speak, or look around. The atmosphere was pretty charged. The constable pushed the statement across. "Soign 'ere."

He was doing his best to keep an even keel, but the going was choppy.

"Now please, Mrs Poindexter," he said desperately.

"Yuv read what my son had to say, officer. It's all been taken down and right in as they say, so I fail to see how yuh can continue to suspect my brother of this foul deed—"

"I say," said Pop. "Foul deed, I say that's rather—"

"Shut up!" said Ma. "It must be painfully obvious to you, officer, that your suspicions are merely a waste of your time and ours. My brother stands without a stain on his character, and has never so much as laid a hand on the property of any local citizen, let alone a fowl."

Uncle Athol began to nod vigorously, but stopped suddenly.

"Ah think, officer, it seems fairly conclusive," Pop began, but tailed off as Constable Ramsbottom leaned back in his chair and surveyed us balefully.

"What about the geh-hurl?" he said hoarsely. "Is the young lady able to add to the teste-mehoney?"

We had all made a statement now except Prudence. I was the only one who had ventured past the point of saying that, when we had retired, Uncle Athol was tucked in for the night. I considered that snoring touch to be masterly.

What with one thing and another, we had all forgotten Prudence was scheduled to turn sixteen the next day, but her legs had not forgotten and neither had her gym frock, which looked startlingly skimpy. Although she had been home from school for more than six months, Prudence still wore her gym frock nearly every day of the week.

She had not said a word all night, just stayed glued up against the end of the mantelpiece, playing soundlessly with a matchbox and now and again pushing back that lock of hair. It was the only corner of the room that was a bit shadowed, over there under the hot-water cupboard, and she looked all legs and cheekbones and eyelashes. I must have recognized then, in a mixed-up sort of way, what I had found puzzling on Saturday when she crossed the street to Les and me, and on Sunday when she had hung down from the beam in the shed. Doggone it, she was grown up and she *was* pretty. Just as Prudence moved away from the mantelpiece looking puzzled and beautiful —yes, beautiful, dirty face and all—our front door bell, which no one had used in years, started to ring and, simultaneously, our back door to knock.

"I'll go," I said. I was starting to feel the strain of sitting there not looking at my uncle, gutless wonder that I was, and my bet is, he was glad to see the back of me too.

Just what do you think when you pull the bolt on one of those old-fashioned front doors, with a couple of miniature church windows in them? The shadow could belong to anyone from the bailiff to an escaped gorilla, but it's— it's Mr Dabney, the undertaker. Anyway I know what I thought of as soon as I had peered out of the door long enough to establish who it was by the brandy fumes— Uncle Athol's false teeth.

Physically speaking, Mr Dabney would have only been a mouthful for an escaped gorilla, but the ape would have probably immediately sat down and beamed around at all present.

"Franky," beamed Mr Dabney, peering past me down the hall.

"Neddy," I corrected.

"Of course it's Neddy, is yuh father there? I'll come right along in and say howdy to yuh father, Franky. It's nice to meet nice people. Great Scott, the lights won't go out all night, Franky, never fret about that, my boy. Just tell yuh father and dear old Athol that Charlie Dabney is without."

"Wontcha come in, Mr Dabney?" I said, following him down the hall. "This way, out here," I said a bit wildly when we went into a bedroom. I did not want him to find the light switch because I knew, with Pop in bed all afternoon, the big flowered chamberpot would be right in the middle of the room with blankets humped up on the floor all around it. I wanted to prevent Charlie Dabney seeing that chamberpot, at all costs, so I did my level best to shepherd him out of the bedroom. I was prepared to haul him out, if necessary. He was not much bigger than me, but he surely was a hard man to out-manoeuvre.

"Where am I? Where am I?" he called. "Is that you, Athol?"

"No, it's me, Ned. Over here, Mr Dabney. This way, Mr Dabney."

"Great Scott, Athol, put the light on. Don't play tricks on me, yuh ole rascal. Yuh know me, yuh ole reprobate. It's Charlie, Athol, ole Charlie."

Fingers fumbled with my face. I grabbed his sleeve.

"Mr Dabney."

"Athol. It's not Athol at all. Great Scott! Marry me, darling. Marry me now, loveliest flower. Must have heard of me. People just dying to meet ole Charlie Dabney. Not a care in the world."

"Mr Dabney, please, you're in the wrong room."

"Not wrong room at*tall*, my precious flower. Wrong attitude, thasall. Wrong attitude altogeth'. Rightroom, insis'. Great Scott, what a smooth skin, what a complexion. Born for love and kisses, my flower. Charlie may be a little old, but he knows a trick or two—"

"C'mon, c'mon," I snarled.

The chamberpot made a gong-like sound as Mr Dabney clipped it with his foot as we waltzed around. I felt an agonizing embarrassment thinking of our guest, Constable Ramsbottom; and then, blow me tight, groping around in the dark I kicked it myself. It made the same sort of mysterious, carrying sound you hear at sea in a fog.

When I got Mr Dabney out to the kitchen and he framed himself importantly in the doorway, he seemed to have dismissed the whole bedroom episode from mind, but I never will. Uncle Athol and Pop promptly gathered around the visitor, but the cop did not even glance at him. Angela Potroz had arrived via the back door and had coyly put a birthday present of the classiest silk stockings, encased in a plastic bag, on the table by the heap of statements. Pru had opened the bag with nervous fingers and Angela was talking to the cop, too excited to recognize him for a fiend in human shape. The cop did not seem to be listening to Angela much. Prudence held up the stockings.

"Oh, Angela. Now I know why you're called Angela. You're an angel, honey."

"Many happy returns."

"Muh very first pair," said Prudence. "Many's the time I've often thought how I'd love a pair of luvlee stockings. Oh, Ma's given me everything yuh wish for, but yuh beat her there."

She was always quick with her soft heart, Prudence. She had seen the way Ma was fluttering around, all grins but with her heart bursting.

"Pop. Pop," said Prudence. "Oh, blow you there then, old Charlie Dabney."

She winked at the cop and Constable Ramsbottom winked back.

"We'll have some supper," said Ma. "I'll put on a quick supper for us all and we'll all feel better. It hasn't been such a bad Monday after all. Nothing like the old cuppa as granny'd say, to brighten us all up. And it's nearly yuh birthday, dear. What a young lady. Kiss your old Ma."

The stove was well out, but we had a gas-ring in the pantry. In that dark little closet, by the light of a candle and the blue flame of the gas-ring, Ma's shadowy bulk and giant, naive heart knocked us up a pot of tea and some mince on toast. I was very surprised to see the mince, as I had no idea there was any in the house. I knew for a fact the tripe and the sausages had all been eaten.

So Constable Ramsbottom had supper with the Poindexters on the noight uv the fifth at the corner of Smythe and Winchester Streets. The moonlight looked askance at the starred windows of the house and poked around among the old stoves and bottles and the ravaged hen-coop and even spared a glance for the old Dennis, which had developed another deflated five-fifty twenty-one.

I will wager that Constable—he was christened Leonard—Ramsbottom had a magic few minutes while Ma was in the pantry and Pop and Uncle Athol and Mr Dabney were taking turns going to the washhouse to knock over a bottle which the alcoholic mortician had smuggled in under his coat. I can see now it was a magic few minutes, but, at the time, I just sat over by the cold stove, a prey to private fears. Prudence and Angela giggled away as Prudence, seated on the edge of the old box ottoman, carefully rolled the sheer silk up her fabulous legs and hooked them on to her school knickers with some suspenders they found in a drawer. I will not go so far as to say I was unaware of these goings on, but puberty was only just marshalling its forces and the trying events of the weekend had deterred the onslaught. Len Ramsbottom was only a rookie cop and a bachelor, and that sister of mine and Angela must have caught him with his hands in his pockets and his mouth hanging open. He was at the ready. The whole bottle and a half of haircream must have been sizzling by the time Ma had the tea and mince on toast ready and Pop and Co. had their attitude restored by the visits to the washhouse.

It does not hurt me to remember Len Ramsbottom having moments, but I wince remembering Prudence slipping her priceless stockings off again with Mr Dabney back in the kitchen. The alcoholic mortician had just been coaxed into getting on the form between the table and the window and he practically had to be held down. He made some fearful insinuations, which Ma, who was up and down all the time, missed, thank heaven; but Prudence could not have been so dumb and suddenly she fixed him with the levellest look imaginable. A dead silence all around went with the look. Then she and Angela went back to semi-flirting with Len Ramsbottom, the heart-throb of the force.

Charlie Dabney was a person it was difficult to imagine really disliking, but for a moment or two he looked at his most unlovable.

Uncle Athol was looking around slyly and sharply and if ever I saw a scamp who was not missing a trick, it was right at that moment.

Pop had three or four tilts at his cup of tea and said, "Good luck" two or three times and then varied it with "Regards". The last toss, Mr Dabney rallied and said "Bon Sonte". Ma ignored them and talked to Len Ramsbottom as if he had brought news from Granny Cudby, God bless her.

"We keep open house, Mr Ramsbottom, open house. We're not rich people, but we're honest. As yuh know now, eh? It's Prudence's birthday tomorrow and no one would be more welcome than yuhself. She's going out to service next week, Mr Ramsbottom, with the nicest people, the Quins, not really service, but looking after things in general. She's been a good girl at school and I would've liked office work for her, but it's so hard to give them a course up at the Tec. Yuh ought to teach her how to type, officer—I mean Mr Ramsbottom."

I had privately consigned Len Ramsbottom to the pigeonhole "lousiest typist ever" and I hid my sour smile by stirring my tea again, but Prudence said, "Oh beauty! Willyuh, Mr Ramsbottom? Willyuh honest, teach me how to type?"

The cop leered at her rosily and waved both hands, including the finger he typed with.

"Course, course," he gurgled. "Course, Miss Poindexter."

She goggled at him. "Cop that, Ma. Hey! I'm Prudence."

I missed a bit of the by-play about now because I went out to the washhouse to try and work out how big a hash of things I had made and just how much "grata" I had gleaned to give Les. The only conclusion I came to was that I was too tired to think.

Mr Dabney had produced another bottle by the time I got back and Pop and he were having a "regards, regards" session. Uncle Athol was keeping as aloof as he could, consistent with getting his glass filled up as regular as clockwork. Ma was being so ultra-hospitable to Len Ramsbottom that Pop and Co. had taken it as the green light and the bottle was slap in the middle of the table.

"Regards," said Mr Dabney. "Great Scott, the lights won't go out all night."

"Regards," said Pop. "Anytime, Charlie, old boy. Always welcome. Come any time at*tall*. Only too pleased. Always on deck. Old Southern hospitality and what have you. Demned poor show if the boys can't compare notes once in a while, what, what. Thank you, thank you, no water, Athol. It's made with water heh, heh, regards. Yes of course. First to agree, old 'man. And how's business? One thing with you, Charlie, customer can't argue back, eh! eh! Heh, heh. Wazzat, wazzat?"

61

"Stiffasaboard. All my clients. Stiffasaboard. Stiff-as-a-board. S-t-i-f-f, yes, yes. Regards old boy. Great gal you got there. Dee-aitch. Great gal. Can yuh hear me, m'dear? Stiffasaboard. Regards, Dee-aitch. Great Scott, she wouldn't do a thing like that in front of me unless realiesh who Charlie Dabney was, eh! eh! Fatal fascination. Always had it. Too fond of the liquor. No regrets. Know a lotta little tricks. Got a pound y'know. Got a pound. Not stuck for a pound, ole boy."

"All businessmen together, Charlie. Tight little town. Tight little town to get a pound in. Lucky to be where we are. Lotta people give their left, er eye, hrmp, sorry Athol, be where we are. Why? Stablished. Thas why. 'Stablished. Regards."

"Yoo-hoo, my dewy rose. Stiffasaboard. Great Scott. Aflame with desire and so on. With passion undiminished, etcetera, etcetera. Dabney, the vagabond lover."

This dewy rose stuff finished me. I felt quite unable to withstand any more of that. I crawled into Herbert's bed by the window. Herbert was always late and we had an understanding. Herbert only had one ambition and that was to prove correct once and for all that a good billiard player really was the outcome of a mis-spent youth. I heard the cop say, "I'll see Miss Potroz home," and I heard Charlie Dabney yoo-hooing away and saying, "Great Scott, the lights won't go out all night." But my lights went out. A guy I have a lot of regard for switched them off at the main.

Chapter Six

THE NEXT DAY was more to be noted in the minds of my buddy, Les Wilson, and myself for a visit from Constable Ramsbottom than because it was Prudence's birthday. After school we were sitting down on boxes by the empty hen-coop (something we were very good at) when the shadow of the Law fell across us.

He joined us cosily, sitting down on the coop itself, and proceeded, forthwith, to ask whether we were or were not going to prefer charges against one described as Athol C. Cudby, for appropriating our joint property, to wit the missing Black Orpingtons.

When my heart stopped free-wheeling I said, no I wasn't. We looked at Les and he said, no, he wasn't, either.

"On the 'ole," said Len Ramsbottom, "Oi think you're woize, very woize. In the hadministration of joostis, occasions aroise when more 'arm than good can be done by prosecuting the mally-factor."

While not getting the full drift of this, I had a feeling I was on his side.

"More 'arm than good," he continued, heavily contemplative. "In this hinstance, the noime of the family must be considered. I 'ave no doubt that yeruncle, in fact he has avowed his intention of so doing to me, will reimburse you for the loss of the purloined poultry."

Just because our mouths fell open he must have thought

we were going to say something for he stayed us with a large palm.

"As an officer of the law it is my duty to apprchend and bring to joostis thuh criminals in our midst. I want it understood that should any further hevidence come to light implicating Cudby, Mr Cudby, in other and more serious crimes a prosecution will himmediately fah-hollow."

"Officer," I said boldly, "have there been other fowls stolen beside mine and Les's?"

"On Saturday, the noight uv the ther-rud, a large-scale robbery was perpetrated at the 'omestead uv Mr Alfred Lynch. A considerable number of pedigree birds, broody resistant, were appropriated and so far there has been no trace uv them."

"Birds?" said Les. "What sorta birds? Budgies?"

"Poultry," came the stern reply. "A number of valuable one-year fowls in full lay, broody resistant. No heffort will be spared to trace the miscreants. Suspicion fell on Cudby, Mr Cudby, because for some weekends past it has come to our knowledge he has been raffling killed and dressed poultry in the bars of local hotels. He avows that, with the exception of your own fowls, he poichased all the birds at Klynham Traders and there is hevidence to support this. In haddition, the hevidence of Mr Lynch seems to point to this particular robbery being perpetrated by younger and more active men."

"How do you mean evidence?" said Les and I.

"The culprits escaped at great speed. Mr Lynch avers that there were possibly two or even three thieves in-volved. Mr Lynch is sure in his own mah-hind that they were young men and very active and fast on their feet. One of them scaled a six-foot fence and the other mem-bers of the gang thought nothing of jumping row after row of goo-hoosberry bushes."

"There must be clues, surely?" I pressed. "Footprints,

fingerprints. Didn't anything get dropped or something?"

"Hunfortunately, nearly the entire neighbourhood turned out and conducted a search uv the garden; and all hevidence, such as footprints, was hobliterated."

"Thank God," said Les. "I mean, good God!"

"What fools!" I contributed hotly. "Why not leave police work to the spechlists? Always some blundering asses around to make it more difficult for the spechlists."

Les was blowing his nose and had his entire countenance covered by his handkerchief, but his ears stuck out like bolshevist flags.

"Never fear," said Len Ramsbottom, rising from the coop. "No heffort will be spared to trace the miscreants."

He cleared his throat and I thought he was going to ask something, but to our relief he moved off. Just as he reached the street, Prudence came galloping around the section of iron fence still standing and banged right into him. He was stooping over putting on a bicycle clip and she staggered him.

I looked at Les, who seemed ill, and I nodded in the direction of the rhubarb. Les nodded back and we folded our tents like a couple of shaky Arabs.

That night we sneaked away from Prudence's party, which was a tame, sissy affair, down to Fitzherbert's shed to give some scraps to the miscreants. Lest this give rise to confusion, I had better explain that it was by this name, since our conversation with the Law, that Les and I thought of the stolen Lynch fowls. In our ignorance and trepidation we had got hold of the wrong end of the stick again.

We made a detour on the way to the shed and got a pack of twenty cigarettes out of the slot machine in the doorway of Thompson's store. Money had suddenly become the least of our worries. Miss Fitzherbert, the tall, mad woman up at the great house, which had pumps, not taps, over the tubs, had told us she would buy all our eggs. It had been Les's idea to approach her and it was a honey. She asked no questions, but she bolted the door when she went for the money; and, the time it took, our guess was it was buried somewhere.

There was no power laid on at the mansion and Les and I could always get a cheap dose of the creeps by sneaking up close at night, through the ancient camellias and magnolias, and glimpsing, through a lofty window, the bent, paralysed figure of the legendary Channing Fitzherbert himself, corpse-like in an honest-to-God four-poster. The lamplight beside the shrivelled dome of a head cast an enormous, vulture-like shadow on the wall. Man, it was horrible. We often did it. One night, through divers landing windows, we saw *her* slowly descending the stairs holding a lamp aloft, and we did not stop running until we made the shed. It was different in the sunlight, standing on the ramp at the back door with the birds twittering in all the old trees and under the eaves, but when night fell the whole lay-out would have tickled Count Dracula pink.

"Miscreants," said Les, surveying by candlelight the fowls roosting on the old gig. "Trust us to pinch something valyoobel."

"I thought they were funny looking," I remarked. "What with those bits of black in the wings and that fluff on their legs."

"Broody resistant," said Les. "But can't the buggers lay!"

The miscreants had settled down to a steady eleven or twelve eggs a day and we were sure of getting two-and-six a dozen. Miss Fitzherbert was buying them all. She must have been preserving them, or something. The old firm of Wilson and Poindexter were on the pig's back, but they shared an uneasy presentiment of their mount turning into a killer mustang without warning. It may have been imagination, but both Les and I had sensed members of the Victor Lynch gang watching us closely at school. We were more apprehensive of trouble from that quarter than from the police, mainly, I think, because Constable Ramsbottom, for all his great bulk, seemed an absolute goof. He made us feel like those master criminals who entertain bowler-hatted yahoos from Scotland Yard and offer them Corona cigars in an inlaid box, in the false bottom of which is the stolen ruby of the Sultan of Yamarramah.

The autumn still of the nights was yielding to a bough-creaking, raindrop-spotted darkness. For all its age, the shed was pretty snug.

"Just who does know about this hideout?" Les asked.

"As far as I know, no one," I said.

"There must be someone."

"Well, I don't count 'Madame Drac'," I said; meaning, by this, Miss Fitzherbert.

"There must be someone, I'm sure."

"Well," I said. "Of course there is. There's Prudence, but shucks, she's O.K."

"Oh yes, Prudence," said Les. "Dang it. Fancy me forgetting Pru."

"As long as no one finds out—" I began.

"You really think Pru's O.K., Ned?"

"Who, Pru? Of course she's O.K. She's just a sheila of course, but she's a good type, old Pru. Once Pop really lammed into her, gave her one helluva hiding, but she never said a word. She came home real late one night, but do yuh think she'd split where she'd been? Not ole Pru."

"Where had she been?"

"How do I know, I never asted her."

After a while Les said, "Well, Ned, this has got me worried a little."

"How come worried? You mean those chooks?"

"No. Pru," said Les. "Being out late like that. Maybe she might have a y'know, a boyfriend. She might have told some boyfriend about the shed."

"Yuh, yuh, yuh," I chortled scornfully. "This was years ago. Pru's got no boyfriend."

"Are you sure, Ned? I meantersay brothers don't know everything."

"Well now that's something I am sure of, Les," I said firmly. "Yuh can get that foolish notion rightouta yuh head. Right clean outa yuh head. We got anuff problems on our hands without you starting to imagine things. Wazzat?"

"Put out the candle," Les mouthed, pointing. I held up a tense finger. The sound came again, but it was only the door straining slightly in a sudden gust.

"Let's fix that window a bit better," Les whispered. "You slip outside and see if yuh can see any light showing and I'll pull the sack over a bit."

"Sure, sure, Les. What say I fix the sack and you go outside and have a looksee?"

"Let's both fix the sack," said Les. "And let's both go outside and have a looksee."

Chapter Seven

"YUH OUGHTA have a bit more sense than that. How'm I to know who's in there if they haven't even got enough sense to shut the door? It looks to me like yuh haven't even got enough sense to yell out when yuh hear somebody coming along the veranda. Anybody can hear somebody coming along this veranda, on account of all these rotten boards, we just not gunna have a veranda on this house for that long if it gets any rottener, so it's silly letting me walk in on yuh like that when all anybody has to do is yell out."

I could not see any occasion for Prudence to be getting so high-hat just because she had surprised somebody in the washhouse, but having a birthday certainly makes a big difference to some people.

"Hi, Neddy," she said to me and went inside the house looking flushed and dusky. She was wearing a torn old frock she had grown out of, and her gleaming mop of hair was tousled. Before she left the veranda she stepped, with one bare foot, on the loose board really hard, going out of her road to do it, and I had to grin because it did not respond nearly as loudly as it did when it got trodden on accidentally. All the boards were sick, but that one had a fever.

Uncle Athol came out of the washhouse and he looked as if he had a fever too. There were two big bright spots on his cheeks like geraniums and his Adam's apple was shooting up and down as if someone were playing tricks with the elevator button. He was not looking like that just because young Prudence was throwing her weight around and growling at him. I had it figured he was crook with the booze as usual. He and I were not on the best of terms, naturally, but I was not going to leave the veranda just because he was there, and it looked as if he intended standing his ground too. He stood staring down the yard at the shed for a while. He kept on fidgeting and he looked very excited about something or other. His shoulders were hunched up and his hands were thrust deep in his trouser pockets. The movement of his fingers as he twiddled them in the lining was plain to see. It began to look as if he were not going to speak at all and the situation was getting more awkward all the time; and then he came around close to me, swallowing hard, and said, "Guess Prudence is right about this veranda being in pretty poor shape."

"Sure is," I said awkwardly.

"I think I'll go across to Sorenson's and borrow a hammer and a few nails. It's beginning to look as if I don't fix that really bad board there, no one's gunna ever do it and someone's gunna break their fool neck on it one uv these fine days. One uv these days a man'll be stepping along without a care in the world and next thing he'll know, he'll be half on the veranda and half under the house. Beats me how that board has stood up as long as it has to the pounding it gets right there, where yuh more or less gotta step on it. If those Sorensons aren't over there at their own house this morning I don't know what I'll do. Number of times I've been over to that place to get a hammer and a few nails and find them out! Beats me where they get to. If they're not over there this morning I'll say to Jim next time I see him, 'Why the hell don't yuh just leave the district and get it over and done with?'

Surely I'll catch them there at home this morning. I'll go across right away and if I can get Jim Sorenson's hammer and a few nails we'll fix that dam' board for good and all. It wouldn't matter if an ole buffer like me, that's had his day, broke his neck, but it worries me to think of one of you youngsters with yuh life in front of yuh, coming a gutzer, and that's what'll happen as sure as Moses hid in the bulrushes."

Having got this off his chest, Uncle Athol went off down our dirt path using the peculiar, spry shuffle which was his characteristic mode of locomotion. I wondered for the hundredth time how a person could answer to the description "spindle shanked and herring gutted" yet still run to a brewer's goitre.

This was Saturday morning and two minutes later I knew I was a marked man. I sauntered out to the street whistling "Roll Along Covered Wagon, Roll Along" and the first thing I saw was the front wheel of a bicycle drawing back out of sight. Someone was sitting on that grid leaning up against the concrete wall of the Temple of the Brethren of the Lamb, which was right opposite our shack across Smythe Street and facing Winchester Street. I went back into the house and up to a front room and peered over the street. I could still see only the front wheel, one handle-bar and a hand, but in a moment or two the stationary rider lost balance and put out a steadying leg on the footpath. It was Skin Hughson, Lynch's right hand man. No doubt about it, he was on the watch. No hood squinting out of a black Cadillac ever struck more fear, no tommygun ever looked more sinister than the propeller on the front mudguard of Hughson's bicycle.

I crawled through a tunnel in the bamboo clump and cut through Grindly's orchard. Between their woodshed and the hedge was a narrow track along which it was possible to squeeze sideways. This brought me out in another backyard, and, once through these people's garage, I would be on the street I was heading for. If I had been one second sooner my little ruse would have been discovered because, just as I slipped through the back door of the garage (the car was out) Peachy Blair went past and only had to look around to have seen me. I could have bashed up Peachy—or Cupid, as some called him—with one arm in a sling, but Peachy was a Lynchite, and this sissy had never copped a thumping at school yet. The plump form was the body of Peachy, but the shadow he cast was the shadow of Victor Lynch and Skin Hughson and Clem Walker and D'Arcy Anderson and Viv Rolands and Don Butcher and Dan and Harold Lowe—in fact the shadow of the gang. His actual function as a member of such a tough bunch was the topic of fascinated whispering. The boys were practising on him, it was said, for the great day when they could procure the genuine article—girls. When that day came the Lynch boys had no intention of showing up as raw beginners. It was all very vague and disturbing but I knew that, to me, Peachy Blair represented the depths of depravity. And because I was puzzled I felt inferior and even more scared. These guys were bad. But *bad*.

I was puffing pretty hard when I slowed down to a walk in Camden Street where Les Wilson lived and maybe that is why I failed to hear the whirr of speeding wheels on the footpath behind me. I let out a staccato yelp of terror when the bicycle skidded to a halt right alongside, so close that one pedal gouged my bare calf. The collision barged me backwards into the hedge. Clem Walker's eyes were gleaming. He was big and powerful, horrible looking, with cropped hair and an abundance of warts and pimples. Another grid came wheeling in off the road ahead of us. A smiling D'Arcy Anderson propped it in the kerb and dismounted. I was a bit jealous of D'Arcy Anderson's good looks and in some twisted way his arrival helped me to put on a better show. If Skin Hughson, say, had been

Clem Walker's companion, I do not think I could have stopped my knees shaking.

"We wanna have a little talk with you, Poindexter," said D'Arcy smiling and standing with his thumbs hooked into his belt.

"Well, can I get outa this hedge, first, please?" I said as angrily as I could.

"Let 'im out, Clem," grinned D'Arcy. It began to look as if D'Arcy ranked higher in the gang than Clem Walker. I suppose that meant he got more turns with Peachy. It made me sick.

My leg was pretty sore and tears were not far away.

"By crummy, that hurt," I said. The blood was running down my leg. "What's the idea, anyway?"

"Hop on the bar of my grid," said D'Arcy. "I'll double you round to meet some pals of ours."

"That'll be the day," I said. "We kin talk here, can't we?"

"We could," said Walker. "But we ain't gunna, see?"

Quick as a flash he grabbed my ear and twisted it. It doubled me over and forced me to my knees. With my eyes swimming with tears, I saw the big, hairy legs and the bicycle tyres and I felt as sick as a pig with life in general.

As I limped over to the grid propped in the gutter, Anderson lashed with his shoe at my rump and I fell on top of the machine, which toppled over. I heard them laughing, and one of them said, "Pick it up." Now both of my hands were skinned as well. I gritted my teeth.

As soon as I realized we were cycling in the direction of Fitzherbert's shed, I knew the game was up.

They dropped the grids in the grass and D'Arcy called out, "We've got Poindexter."

To me he said, "In yuh get."

Lynch himself was in the shed, and the Lowe twins, Dan and Harold.

73

"Nice work," said Lynch. "Cut down and call off the boys, D'Arcy. Tell 'em to get up here as quick as they can."

Victor Lynch got off the benzine box he was sitting on. He kicked one of the miscreants, which was picking away at the ground by his feet.

"Well, yuv got yourself real trouble this time, Poindexter," he said.

"What's the idea? I haven't done anything."

"Don't waste yuh breath," said Lynch. "We've been watching you and Wilson come backwards and forwards to this shed ever since these fowls were stolen from my Pater. There isn't much goes on in this town we don't know about. Yuh can go to jail for this, Poindexter."

I decided the best thing was to say nothing at all. I was right in the cart.

"Instead of going to the police, we're gunna handle this ourselves. Have yuh got an idea what that means?"

"Shall I tickle'm up a bit and make'm talk, Vic?"

"Just a little, maybe."

I had always rated myself as strong for my age, but Clem Walker was way out of my class. He whipped his arms up under my armpits and whacked my chin down on my chest. My knees buckled and next thing I was getting a worm's eye view of what the miscreants were doing in their spare time. I don't know what they hit me on the temple with, but I have always thought of it as a big knot on the end of a rope. There had been a weapon of this nature kicking around the shed for a long time. I never saw it after this. Walker eased off the full-Nelson and I rolled over on the dirt floor. It seemed like pain was the express and hatred was a little puffing billy and they met full on. Me, I was sitting on a jigger between them. Voices. Someone hooked an arm under my neck and I sat up. A lot of feet. I thought I was going to vomit.

74

The pain in my head made me feel really ill. I stared at the ground. Our old shed.

"Want another belt, Poindexter?" said Lynch.

"No," I said.

"Then get up—get the crybaby up on his feet, Clem."

When they forced me up on my feet I rocked to and fro rubbing my temple.

Lynch said softly, "Come over and sit here on this box, Ned."

The box was like a feather bed.

After a while Lynch said, "We're only just starting to work on you, ole boy. We're going to beatcha up and beatcha up—every day. There isn't anything you can do. Every day we're going to get yuh and bash yuh up, old boy. Really bash yuh up."

Silence and a lot of feet. Some more of the gang barged into the shed, but got signalled to shut the door quietly.

"Unless," said Lynch, and I heard a sort of sigh go around, "unless you're prepared to corporate with us, ole boy."

I heard the sigh go around the shed again. I think all the Lynchites must have been there by this time.

"We bin thinking," said Lynch. "We're got the idea you'd make a pretty good member of this gang. How'd yuh like to join the gang, Ned?"

"Gee," I said.

"There's only one condition and it's one that might just surprise you. We need a girl in this gang, to give us a bit of class. We're the most pow'ful gang in the town, but it seems to us we need a real pretty girl like your sister Prudence to give us a bit of class. Now how about that, Ned? You and Prudence join up with us and we'll have the town beat. We'll have everything."

"Oh boy," said Peachy. "Oh boy, oh boyoboyoboy—"

"*Shut up*. Now that's the condition I want to put to

you, Ned. You ask Prudence to join us. You bring her along here about three o'clock this afternoon and we'll join yuh both up with the most pow'ful gang in town. We'll forget all about bashing you up, if yuh think yuh kin bring yuh sister Prudence along to this shed this afternoon. Now that seems to me to be a pretty fair offer, Ned. More'n fair."

"Sure. Sure. I reckon if I ask Prudence to come along, it'll be O.K."

Someone whistled softly. The Lynchites started slapping each other's backs and punching arms. Peachy started jumping around all over the shed.

"We'll leave Wilson outa this," Lynch grinned. "Do him and yuhself a good turn, Neddy, and leave him on the out. Yuh understand. I don't want us to find out yuh been even talking to him. For both yuh sakes."

D'Arcy Anderson walked a couple of blocks with me not saying much and just waving casually when he mounted his grid and rode off. My thoughts, now I was alone, were muddled and miserable as I walked. What a long street! Without any dinner and a throbbing lump on my temple, it certainly looked a long street.

When I went past Les Wilson's place I took a quick look up and down the street and made a dive for it. Les was feeding his little sister on the back steps when he saw me come pelting around and he looked embarrassed. He could see it was an emergency so he dumped the kid and we went into the woodshed.

"I'm a member of the Victor Lynch gang," I said, playing it tough and straight. I told him how they had hailed me that morning. I showed him my lump. "Now look, Les," I said, "yuh got to pretend me'n you're enemies now. Unless I do what this crowd say I'm in for it good and proper. I told them O.K., I'd join on condition they left you alone and of course me too. They said if I joined no one was gunna hurtcha. All the same I'd keep outa their road, if I wuz you. Now, look, Les, yuh know I'm no traitor. I've gotta do this, just gotta do it, and all the time I'll be spying on 'em. Soon we'll know all their secrets and then look out."

"But whadda they want yuh for?" said Les. "Whadda hell they want *you* in the gang for?"

It was pretty insulting, but it was too good a point to just shrug off. Les did not look very happy. He kept looking at my stomach, instead of my face.

"I dunno, Les," I said helplessly. "They must want me to do something, I s'pose. Don't ask me what it is, 'cause I don't know. Look, Les, we'll have to work out a system of seeing each other at night, somehow. Yuh can't come around to our place 'cause I'm a cert to be watched. I'll have to sneak around here when I've got some news."

"I don't care what they say," said Les. "That's our shed."

"Don't be a mad fool," I told him. "I tell yuh they were all in the shed this morning. They know all about it. For Chrissake don't go near the shed. I know how yuh feel. I feel the same way, but we'll beat this bunch, somehow."

"Aren't yuh goin' to the pitchers this afternoon?" said Les. "What about 'The King of Diamonds'?"

He could not have said anything to make me feel worse. But I knew now I had to get going to catch Prudence in case she was going to the cinema. The funny way Les was taking it did not make me feel any happier about what I was going to have to say to Prudence. Come to face it, what was I going to say? All the way to our place I tried out different approaches. I decided on something along these lines.

"Pru, you've got to help me. We've always been pals, Pru. They're real wild about those fowls and it wouldn't surprise me if they go to the police and then I'll go to Borstal. That'll really knock old Ma. All they want is for you to join the gang, Pru. They've got an idea a pretty girl is just what they want in the gang. They reckon you're

77

the prettiest girl in Klynham. They all reckon that, the prettiest by far. They're not bad guys really, there's D'Arcy Anderson and the Lowe boys and all, they only want you to join up and they'll forget all about us pinching the chooks."

This is just about what I did say too.

"What about Les?" said Prudence, rubbing some butter on my lump.

"Les is out of it for now, ouch," I said. "All they want is me'n you. They're the most pow'ful gang around, Pru. It's not going to do any harm giving it a go and I'm gunna be in for a lot of trouble if yuh don't come along this afternoon. Be a sport, Pru. It'll be a lot of fun, I reck'n. Ouch."

"Who said I was the prettiest girl in town?" Prudence asked. "Sounds like a lotta bull to me."

"No, fair dinkum. They all said yuh were. That's why they reckon yuh ought to belong to the most pow'ful gang in the town."

"But I'm older'n them. They're just a bunch of kids."

"Hey, come off it. You're only a year older'n me."

"Nearer two years, boy."

"Well, awright, but half these guys are older'n me. Aw c'mon, Pru, I tell you they're gunna give me the works over those chooks if we don't join up."

"That's your funeral," she said, putting the butter away. "O.K. What am I s'posed to wear, and if I don't like their style I'll tell yuh something, Neddy, if they start fooling around any, my name's Goff and I'm off."

Now Prudence had agreed, my worries should have been on the way out, but I felt miserable and a heel. I had smelt a big rat all along about their wanting Prudence to join the gang, but I had just shut it out of my mind. When she spoke of them fooling around, as she put it, I thought about Peachy Blair and the looks the Lynchites had exchanged among themselves when I agreed, to save my

78

own skin, to talk my sister into coming along down to the shed. They were going to fool around that was for sure. I was forced to admit it to myself at last and I felt pretty sick.

Saturday mornings were always bright and noisy and I never hear sausages sizzling without remembering them, but once the last plate had clattered in the rack over the sink, it was afternoon and peaceful. Pop and Uncle Athol had taken off in the Dennis. Herbert was in town with his 18 oz. sweetheart, looking on the cloth while it was green. The tap was running in the washhouse where Ma was. Dolly and Monica were around somewhere playing with their rag doll.

The autumn sunshine had no zip in it, but it was warm in the kitchen. The door was open, admitting a pathway of yellow light, and when the loose board on the veranda went ker-lunk a big shadow fell right across the room. Prudence stepped sideways to see who it was, manifested great surprise, and said "Good-dayee, come on in."

In came Len Ramsbottom with a silly smirk and his portable typewriter. He looked even more embarrassed than Les had when I caught him feeding the baby. I felt as sick as a pig myself at the sight of the big cop. He started in talking about how he was just on his way past and suddenly remembered promising Prudence some typewriting lessons. It did not seem possible that a big fellow like him had actually become infatuated with my sister, but what were you supposed to think when he blushed like that? Come to think of it he only looked like an overgrown boy, dressed as he was in open-necked shirt and sports clothes. Suddenly I wished I was as big as that. With those shoulders I could wade into the Lynchites and skittle them right, left and centre. If only I could say, "Look, Mr Ramsbottom, would you help me?" But that was out. Overgrown boy or not he was still a cop. Lynch had me over a barrel.

"Harpas' two," I said meaningly, and gave Pru one of

those looks, but she ignored me and sat up behind the typewriter at the table, too excited to heed her brother in his plight.

"Oi have some foolscap 'ere, which we insert into the machine thus," said the young cop. Insert into the machine thus!

I went into the bedroom and sat on Herbert's bed. Save for one amber shaft of autumn sunlight in which dust shimmered and danced, it was dark in here, particularly after sitting in the kitchen. I recalled a saying of Ma's which went, "Oh, well, I s'pose it'll all be the same in fifty years' time." Anyone who has ever had occasion to say something like this to himself will appreciate how low I was feeling and what a great spiritual boost the afore-mentioned saying can be. In a pig's eye it can be.

But after a while Prudence called out to me: "Neddy, it's getting on for three. You better scoot down to Connie's place and tell her I'll be there'n 'bout half 'n hour."

What a sister in a million! And yours truly was leading her by the hand into a gang of thugs that took turnabout at Peachy Blair. I knew it was Prudence's way of telling me she would come on down to the shed as soon as she could to meet the gang, but I was in such a stew, I was half-way to Connie's place before I woke up and altered the tiller. I think I hinted at this before, but Connie is our married sister who got in the family way to that rail-road man, Jim Coleman.

By four o'clock it was one of those silent, dark after-noons when people burn leaves.

"Quite sure she's coming O.K., Poindexter?" D'Arcy said, pitching away his fag end. "I wouldn't like to think of you making a mistake, y'know. You bin telling us for over an hour how your sister is coming, but no sign, no sign. How come?"

I smiled toughly. "She's coming, Ander—" I hoped he

thought I had said Andy. I had wanted to call him Anderson, but choked on it.

"Let's get back up to the gang," said D'Arcy. He gestured debonairly for me to precede him. I sauntered up over the path. It was odd how my jealousy of D'Arcy's good looks gave me a certain aplomb.

When we re-entered the shed Don Butcher and Peachy were standing close together in the middle of the floor. Don Butcher jerked his head around, but when he saw it was D'Arcy and me he put his hand back down Peachy's trousers. My sitting-in-the-hay feeling gave a violent kick and then expired altogether.

"No sign of Prudence?"

"He guarantees she'll be along," D'Arcy told Lynch. Lynch nodded. He seemed interested in what Don Butcher was doing to Peachy. I had trouble knowing where to look. I was unable to shut Peachy's giggling out of my ears.

"Don't be rough, Don," I heard the giggling voice. "Thas nice. Oo you're making me all silly. Stop it now, you'll puckeroo me for Prudence."

"Shut up." A kind of roar went around the shed. But it was too late. I had heard. Now I could not fool myself any longer.

"Wanta feel, Neddy?" said Lynch.

"Go on. Give old Peachy a feel up."

Peachy was jumping up and down. He started to run off around the shed and then he stopped dead, buckled up and sank down on his knees.

"Quick, quick," he yelled. "Ask me sumpin'. Gimme a sum."

"Twenty-five and twenty-five?" Don Butcher shouted.

"Fifty," yelled Peachy.

"A hundred and a hundred."

"Tunhred."

"Six 'n eighteen," screamed Harold Lowe. They were all mad with excitement.

"Shut up. Shut up," said Peachy, in a happy, sing-song voice. "I'm O.K. now. It's gone back. I'm O.K. now for Prudence." He sank over on his rump with his arms stretched out behind him and his hands on the floor and looked stupidly at his plump, smooth legs.

"Neddy wantsta feel yuh up," sneered Lynch.

"Not ye-et," said Peachy. He looked up at me coyly. "Soon, Neddy."

"I can wait," I said to D'Arcy.

"He can wait," sneered Don Butcher and gave me a quick, playful punch in the stomach. They all laughed and jumped around.

"Look at the sissy, he's howling."

"Leave him alone," snapped Lynch. "Haven't any you guys got any brains? You O.K., Ned?"

"I'm O.K.," I gulped. "That joker doesn't know his own strength."

They made a lot of this and went on repeating it as if it was the funniest thing they had ever heard.

"Doesn't know his own strength."

"You don't know yuh own strength, Don. Huh, huh."

"Good ole Samson."

"He's not Sampson," Peachy suddenly yelled, getting up off the floor. "He's SIMPSON."

He went leaping all over the shed smacking himself on the backside.

"SIMPSON, SIMPSON, SIMPSON."

He tripped over one of the scuttling miscreants. He saved himself from falling and managed to grab the poor confused bird between his ankles. He squatted down over it. "I'm a rooster," he yelled, going through the motions. "I'm a bloody great randy rooster."

Everyone was having hysterics at Peachy's antics on the squawking fowl and I was grinning away with murder in my heart when a hand grabbed me by the throat and rammed me back against the wall.

"Where's yuh sister?"

"I dunno," I said. All I could see was Lynch's eyes and the rafters. What a lot of cobwebs!

In my daydreams I had always been able to beat the daylights out of Lynch. I had not realized, just because he was shorter, how much more solidly built he was. Now I knew my daydreams were letting me down with a bump again. And I knew why Lynch was the boss. He hit me and my head hit the wall. He must have hit me a couple more times on the way down, but it was no fist that broke my rib. A boot did that. By my black-and-blue condition, nearly all over my body, they must have all had a turn at putting in the boot.

I put on a great act of being dead and I really thought it had gone across because the Lynchites were so deadly quiet. Without knowing it, I must have been right out the Joe a long time because the silent feet I thought surrounded me were not feet at all, but the miscreants in a very subdued frame of mind. We had Fitzherbert's shed to ourselves. It was cold and beginning to get dark.

Chapter Eight

S UNDAY, as just related, makes a grim and depressing
memory, but I look back on the subsequent fortnight
wistfully. It was the first time in my life I had ever stayed
away from school for more than an a.w.o.l. afternoon and
I suppose that is what lends the reminiscence its sweetness.
Retrospect seems to have a tendency to gloss over the
miserable aspects. The first week I was in real pain. Dr
Mahoney wrapped a bandage around my ribs so tightly it
was as bad as a lorry wheel on my chest.

The worst part of it was I had caught a snorter of a
cold. Sneezing was bad enough, but when the phlegm
moved down on my chest it was murder. I tried lying on
my face, getting on my knees beside the bed, standing up
with my hands pressing my side, but every cough was still
torture. Half-way through the week Dr Mahoney came
again and wrote out a prescription for a concoction to
break up the congestion. He did not come again and we
were secretly relieved at this because there was no Social
Security in those days and every time Ma and I heard the
quack's car door slam and those squeaky tan shoes approaching, it only meant one thing, ten and sixpence. Oh,
and of course, was the room tidy? Dr Mahoney was very
bluff and nice to Ma and me and he did not seem to hold
against us one little bit that mortifying time when he had
been called out in the middle of the night to attend Uncle

Athol whose mysterious ailment turned out to be ye olde fashioned dingbats.

The way Uncle Athol had performed that night was something awful and by his bubbling moans we had all expected him to pass over, but Dr Mahoney had really read him the riot act.

"Get back into bed, you old fool," I can hear Doc saying. "You're not going to die, more's the pity. You're silly with the plonk, that's your trouble, Cudby."

It always embarrassed me dreadfully the way Pop seemed to lack the sense and pride just to say "Good day" to Doc, instead of trying every time to bail him up and talk importantly. Dr Mahoney used to just brush Pop aside, ignore him, but every time the two men met Pop would have another go. He never did get further than clearing his throat and commencing, "Speaking of course purely as a layman—"

Hanging around the house most of the time, cooped up in my room, and getting spoilt that fortnight, my speed-ometer clocked over. "Come on, Neddy," nature whispered. "You're a big boy now, don't let the team down."

This doll, Josephine McClinton, I have mentioned earlier, had the real honour of setting the ball rolling. Now the weather was getting wintry she had started wearing long stockings, sometimes black, sometimes brown (I knew every pair) but her frocks were not any longer and when she rode her bicycle down Smythe Street to her music lessons (she must have learned from the sisters at the Convent, I think, not the alcoholic and doomed Mabel Collinson) four o'clock on Tuesdays and five o'clock on Fridays, returning three-quarters of an hour later, I never even saw her supercilious expression, but only the exciting short stretch of leg between her pants and her garters. Conditions for this spectacle on Fridays were not ideal, because the days were drawing in and it was too dark to get a good eyeful of her on her way back. Not only that but it was tea-time and the family were all in and out of my room, curse them. One Tuesday I had a real orgy. Josephine stopped to yarn to another girl on the street, directly outside my window. The subject of their respective stockings must have cropped up, because I have never seen such a leg show since. Well, I have, I guess, but not with such shuddering impact. I was crouched down by the window in the bedroom, but if I had been out behind the old stove in the yard it would not have surprised me to see smoke coming out of it. My blood was simmering like an Irish stew. To make things worse a pile of old magazines about film stars and such had been dumped on me to read and they were loaded with pictures of absolute honeys with practically nothing on. If I could have gone for a run around the block, or something, I might have weathered the storm (for storm it was), but cooped up like that I was a gone coon.

"Herbert," I croaked, in the small hours of one morning. I had lain awake waiting for him to come home, but had lacked the courage to speak until the light was out.

"Go sleep," mumbled Herbert.

"Herbert," I repeated. He must have twigged the crack in my voice because there was a sound as if he had propped himself up on one elbow.

"Herbert," I said. The crack in my voice was a crevasse by this time. He came over and sat on my bed or his bed, have it any way you like, and put his hands on my shoulder with the tips of his fingers spread out as if he were hard up against the cush.

"Wassa trouble, kid?"

I told him all about what I was up to and how, no matter how hard I tried, I could not help myself. "I'll go blind. I'll die," I concluded.

"Stop crying," said Herbert.

He went back to his bed to get a handkerchief from under his pillow. He blew his nose and lit a cigarette.

86

"Stoppit, willyuh?" he said. "Cut it out and listen to yeruncle 'Erb."

I listened and I was a lucky boy to have asked a pimply-faced character like Herbert whose only God was a hundred break. One kid I heard of was so stricken with grief and worry he asked a minister and a week later he hung himself in the washhouse. The kid, I mean.

I held on to Herbert's hand in the dark, but in the end we broke it up and got some shuteye.

I think Prudence felt pretty bad about me getting beaten up on account of her not turning up at the shed that Sunday, but I refrained from rubbing it in and, what with her starting work for the Quins and me with my new problems, nothing much was said. Incidentally Ma thought my rib got broken wrestling.

Les came around to see me one night in the first week I was sick and I had a feeling he was ashamed of himself for having thought of me as a traitor. He could see now, or thought he could, that I had taken the knock for both of us. I explained to him about Prudence and how I had bluffed the Lynch gang that she was coming when all the time she knew nothing about it. I just about had myself bluffed by this time.

"The dirty sods," Les said, horrified. "What were they gunna do to her, Ned?"

"You-know," I told him, thinking about Josephine McClinton.

"The dirty sods," said Les. "You mean they were gunna, you-know?"

"Thas right," I nodded. "But hang on, listen, until I tell you about Peachy Blair."

He listened and commented as follows.

"The dirty sods."

"If yuh ask me thas not all they do, either."

"You mean—they you-know?"

"Thas right."

"The dirty sods."

Les began to come around nearly every night to have one of our increasingly ignorant and filthy (but delightful) bedside chats about "you-know" and one night I woke up to the fact that he was carrying a torch for my big sister. It seemed incredible, but there it was. Prudence came home from the Quins' about eight o'clock each night and as soon as we heard her voice and her laugh out in the kitchen, Les's end of the conversation went haywire and his ears got pink. She was Les's Josephine McClinton! Well how about that? My big sister! That is what she had become as soon as she started work. My big sister! It might have just been the effect of wearing shoes, but she seemed to have sprouted, her legs seemed longer. Prudence was very slender—willowy might be a better adjective—but she had the meat in the right places and it seemed to quiver when she strutted about.

Les made a bit of an ass of himself one night by coming to light and asking me if I thought he ought to keep an eye on Prudence in case the Lynchites were still after her.

"Don't make me laugh," I said. "What could *you* do? Pru can look after herself."

"Well, I just thought—"

"Besides," I added, nastily, "if yuh ask me she's got a policeman for a boyfriend now."

"How d'yuh mean?" asked Les, looking so confused I felt sorry for him.

"Oh, I dunno, really, but this cop that came around about Uncle Athol is always hanging around giving her typewriting lessons. Came last night after you'd gone home. Ask me, he only types with one finger himself."

"But he's a grown-up man," protested Les. "And a cop too. It can't be right."

It was the way I felt too, but I stuck to my guns.

"He looks like a bull," mumbled Les.

"Maybe that's what these sheilas like," I said, feeling

nearly as sick and confused as Les looked to be.

"A prize bull," said Les viciously.

"A prize prick, anyway," I amended vulgarly.

It was Prudence herself who routed our speculations. She came into the bedroom one night. Les sprang off his chair and offered it to her, but she flopped down on one of my feet.

"Hey," I yelled. "That's my foot in case you don't know. Watch out where you stick your bum on my bed."

I only spoke in this crude fashion to show off in front of Les. I wanted to make it quite clear to Les that, as far as I was concerned, Prudence was still only the kid I had once tipped up and forced to eat boot polish.

"You're late home, tonight," I sneered. "Been stepping out with ole—" I employed the pet name we had for Len Ramsbottom.

"To whom do you refer by that vulgar remark?" said Prudence haughtily.

To whom do you refer? What next!

"My dear little brother," said Prudence, who knew damn' well to whom I did refer. "My deah, deah, little brother." She addressed the air and Les. One half of her audience, anyway, had the sense not to snigger away like an idiot.

"Don't hand me that stuff," I went on. "Don't try and kid me he only just about lives here to give yuh lessons on that old typewriter. If yuh could type with two fingers yud be twice as good as him, huh, huh. If yuh could type with three fingers yud be three times as good, huh, huh, huh."

I glared at Les, expecting to get some appreciative mirth out of him, but he just sat on the edge of his chair, simpering.

"Ask me," I said darkly, "he's out to teach yuh more than just typewriting."

"Just what," said Prudence, "d'yuh mean by that remark, Neddy Poindexter?"

"You know," I said, and Les's ears pricked up. This was sailing pretty close to the wind.

Prudence, lock of dark, wavy hair over one eye, was leaning back with her hands stretched behind her, palms down as support, and she was showing a lot of leg, so it is my guess Les was only pretending to look at the floor, but I was in no state to censure him for that, not the way things were.

"Constable Ramsbottom is being very kind to give me lessons on his typewriter," Prudence said firmly. "And that is all there is to it, I'll have you know. However, I will say he has very nice wavy hair."

"Yuh, yuh," I jeered.

"But not as nice," said Pru, blushing, "as someone else I know."

This shut me up and I guess it registered with Les too. That authentic note is quite unmistakable. Prudence shook the bang of hair out of her eye and looked all dreamy.

"Hey," I said. "Yuh got a ladder in the new stockings that Angela gave yuh."

That jolted her.

"Where? Oh!"

She leaned forward and pulled back her skirt an inch or so with the tips of her fingers and stood up quickly.

"I'll put some soap on it," she announced. Les looked up at her like a spaniel pup. It made me sick.

Just before she went out the door she stopped and looked at Les.

"Who's the young man atcha pa's store?" she asked.

"Who?" said Les with a start. "Clarrie Homes."

"No, the new boy. The tall one with the, ahem, curly, fair hair?"

"Oh him," said Les. "He's just started. The fat guy?"

"He's not so fat," said Prudence indignantly.

"If Les says he's fat—" I began.

"Chester Montgomery," said Les.

"He's fat," I concluded.

Prudence repeated the name.

"What a name!" I said. "Is that a name?"

Prudence screwed her nose up at me as she went out. Then she poked her head back into the room for a minute and said, "Well, I think he's rather nice."

"Who is he?" I asked Les, hoarsely.

"The new chap Dad's taken on at the store. Honestly Neddy, he's fat. Y'oughta see him riding the store bike. He's really fat, Ned. And he's a drip. He's got a squeaky voice. Y'oughta see the way he dances around and kids up to the customers when he's behind the counter. He's like a big, fat, bumblebee in a bottle. I heard Dad tell Mum he overdoes being polite. It's ness'ry to be polite, Dad says, but he said to Mum that this new guy lays it on a bit thick. According to my father it's ness'ry to be polite in a store, but yuh don't want to overdo it, neither. According to my father this Chester bloke is the most polite guy he's ever seen. Just wait till you go into the store, Neddy I wouldn't be surprised if this Chester Montgomery is the politest guy in the world."

"How old is he?"

"Hard to tell, eighteen or nineteen, I s'pose. He's not as old as the copper bloke, that's one thing, but boy, he's twice as polite, that's fuh sure."

"You're a bit keen on Prudence aren't you, Les," I said, so suddenly it even surprised me.

"Well, Neddy," said Les awkwardly, "since you must know, I s'pose I am just a bit. Just a little bit."

"Well, don't look so ashamed," I said. "I'm on your side, Leslie. Looks like we don't have to worry about this cop any more. Now our problem is this Montgomery character. According to what yuh say I just can't understand Pru going overboard for a clown like that. From what yuh tell me he's a real booby."

"He is, Neddy," Les avowed. "He is, dinkum."

"Then maybe he's not our problem at*tall*," I said, the shadow of the sick-bed lending me mystical insight.

"How d'yuh mean?" worried Les.

"Maybe Prudence is," I told him.

Ma kicked Les out early these nights and gave me a cup of warm milk. Then I was supposed to go to sleep. Instead of that, I nearly developed astral powers. I nearly learned the secret of projecting my spirit through the night to have "you-know" with Josephine McClinton, the while relaying the seventh heaven of its sensations back to me, the master, snug and relaxed in my own bed. This is something I am sure Herbert, wise as he was, had never thought of. This remote-control invention of mine involved falling asleep and yet not falling asleep. It involved thinking of precisely nothing except some specific conception of "you-know" until my spirit went wheeling away on its lecherous travels. It took a lot of concentration, believe me, and it never worked. It never worked because of the karaka-tree. For years the karaka-tree had scraped and banged in the wind against the bit of our iron fence that still stood; and, with every bang, the fence leaned further over the narrow sidewalk along Smythe Street. I had become so used to this sound that it was just a part of the night. It was not a sound which could have ever kept me awake; and yet, just when I had nearly mastered this new, mysterious power and the darkness was beginning to go ecstatically up and down, up and down, the movement lost its identity and became a sound instead—the sound of that confounded scraping and banging karaka-tree.

Chapter Nine

THE STAIRWAY up to Mabel Collinson's studio was as sharp and quivering as a chord on a cool vibrophone. One step inside the doorway, one step along the passage, and bang!—there was the staircase, steep as a fire escape.

The high, narrow, box-like building was as old as the town itself. It was at the very end of the main street, on the dawn side of the elm. Mabel Collinson had lost all but six of her piano pupils through breathing gin fumes and cigarette smoke over them, and, at her lowest ebb, making daring suggestions to adolescent boys. She was a beautiful pianist, and had won an open scholarship when she was ten years old. At thirty-six, her body was still youthful and lovely like that of Dorian Gray, but her face was the tell-tale painting in the attic. She laughed like hell when she lost a pupil because that night there were always midnight footsteps, flask at hip, hauling their way up those bloody stairs. At ten o'clock one morning when a very frightened Mabel was feeling so ill she thought maybe she was going to die, she fell down those bloody stairs and broke her neck. This is what killed her of course, but actually she died of everything.

When Mabel Collinson played her Lipp piano late at night, her only audience was Sam Finn, the local halfwit. Every night he came and sat, across the road from Mabel's place, on a gate which opened into a paddock.

The beautiful music entranced him and filled his simple heart with wonder. He hated the loud voices of the few late wayfarers who, heedless of the music, walked home along the middle of the pale road that ran past the old frame building like a stream. When the piano ceased to play and the light went out upstairs, Sam Finn would climb down from the gate and go peacefully back to his little shack and crawl into a brass bedstead beside his syphilitic, methylated-spirit-drinking uncle.

Although on the day of Mabel's tragic fall Sam Finn gathered in his hazy way that something dreadful had occurred, he felt deeply that it was wrong for the beautiful music to cease and that, accordingly, it would still be somewhere. When the hours passed and still no light appeared upstairs, Sam Finn climbed sadly down from the gate. He knew that when lights went mysteriously out and blinds were drawn, people had often moved to Mr Dabney's place, so he went on to the funeral parlour.

He stood for a long time in the dark alley between the Federal Hotel and Mr Dabney's parlour, but, although he strained his ears listening, he could hear no sound of music. There was a light, however. It moved about behind the high, Gothic, richly-dight windows of the chapel like a will-of-the-wisp.

In the end, Sam Finn's curiosity would be denied no further. Agile as a monkey, he hauled himself up and stood tip-toe on a window-sill to peer within.

Mabel Collinson had always looked like a goddess to Sam Finn. Whenever he had seen her in the street he had turned and followed her along, making inarticulate sounds and pointing her out to people. One dark afternoon when a fine mist-like rain was falling he had followed her up and down the main street pointing out her silk-sheathed legs, wobbling on high heels, to grinning shoppers; and that night he had taken off all his clothes and lain in the wet grass behind the gate and let the music of her piano, and the fine rain which still persisted, fall on him like a benediction.

To see her now, her head oddly askew, quite unclothed except for a nightdress pulled up above her breasts, sprawling beside a narrow box in the guttering light of a candle and with a trouserless man, a scarecrow of a man whose great, jutting nose cast a shadow like a cliff, crouching over her, fondling her, was more than Sam Finn could bear. Emitting an animal cry he hammered against the stout glass. Sobbing and snarling, he slid to the ground and began to hammer angrily against the door of the chapel Upstairs in the Federal Hotel people moved uneasily in their sleep, but even when the clouds drifted on from the chimneypots and the yellow moonlight flooded their room, they did not awaken. No one heard the blood-curdling cry from the building across the alley Or nearly no one. A timid housemaid at the Federal saw and heard something but said nothing at the time. She later told Prudence. And Prudence is my unsung collaborator in this history.

Mabel's mother, who had been married three times since she had been a Mrs Collinson, had an uncanny experience that night and it lost nothing in the telling. She lived in Sydney, over a thousand miles away across the sea, and had not received news of her daughter's death. She heard the baby grand piano in her lounge being played and it certainly was not her stepson playing boogie-woogie. It was hard to say just what sort of music it was. The weird melody stopped when, with shivers running up and down her spine, she flung open the lounge door.

"I know you don't believe me," she wailed on many an occasion from then on, "but it was Mabel. I just know it was Mabel. Poor, silly Mabel come back as a ghost to tell me she loved me and was sorry. She used to practise all day until I thought she'd drive me up the wall. I'll never sleep alone in that place again."

Sam Finn put up no fight at all. It may well be that his ghost was just as ignorant as the flesh-and-blood Sam and had no idea how to set about a haunting campaign. He had been known to disappear for weeks at a time before, and everyone, including the police, agreed that he must have done it again. It was the full moon, they observed. They recalled that his previous disappearances had always coincided with the full of the moon. Sam Finn's uncle was secretly relieved as the days passed and Sam remained on the missing list, for he now had the brass bedstead all to himself.

Constable Ramsbottom and a little man from the Pensions Department went and interviewed Sam's uncle. The tin shack was in a section not far from the railway station. The grass was nearly up to the roof. Around the doorway the grass was greasy with fat and urine. They extracted no information from Sam's uncle, who leaned in the doorway, red-eyed, but they left something behind. The little man from Pensions was sick. This is why they failed to carry out their duty and search the shack. As it happened it did not matter. Sam Finn was not there. He was never found.

Out in the pot-holed grass lane behind the railway station they breathed in the blended smell of locomotive smoke and cattle-wagons, as if it were attar-of-roses.

"Although Oi say this as shouldn't," observed Constable Len, "if Oi were Sam Finn Oi would continue to in-ker-rease the distance between moiself and moi last domicile with hevery hour that pah-hasses."

The account of Mabel Collinson's fatal accident reached the corner of Smythe and Winchester Streets by noon of the same day, but it was long after I recovered from my broken rib that I learned of Sam Finn's disappearance. In the same way as everyone else, I soon dismissed the information from mind.

The thing I was unable to dismiss from mind was the

horrible story that began to circulate around Klynham. Mabel Collinson, such was the burden of the grim tale, had climbed out of her coffin in the night. Everyone wanted to believe it despite their horror. The fact that Charlie Dabney's consumption of brandy had gone up a bottle a day in his agitation substantiated the story but also undermined it. There was always someone in the whispering group who was inclined to look sceptical. Then came the hysterical letter from Sydney, signed by Mabel Collinson's mother and addressed to the Mayor of Klynham. The Mayor was seen with Charlie Dabney. People playing euchre forgot whose deal it was.

I tried not to think of Lynch and Co. while I was marooned at home, but as the time approached when return to the workaday world was inevitable I began to get frightened. It was no use deluding myself there was not a strong possibility they were still vengeance bent. Les had made a cautious reconnaissance of Fitzherbert's shed and the fowls had gone. There was no sign, he told me, that the shed was being used by the gang. Les himself had, so far, escaped retribution. One thing anyway, I reflected, was that as time passed the chance of the police being informed grew less, and, consequently the hold the gang had on me weakened. I was beginning to build a certain confidence in my own ability to bluff and I mentally took part in many dramatic sessions with the police, and sometimes the headmaster, in judicial capacities, and my glib tongue invariably worsted the Lynchites. Looking at things in the perspective which the long hours of leisure granted to me, I could see that their demands on Prudence had given me a trump card to play, and an ace at that. It put the enemy in a very bad light and made me out a real hero going through the agonies of hell with a stiff upper lip, for his sister's sake.

As my daydreams got really back into their stride, I frequently thrashed Victor Lynch and sometimes Lynch

and D'Arcy Anderson at one and the same time. One afternoon the frenzy of my imagination was such that I
stumbled around the room lashing out and flattening
nearly the entire Lynch gang, one after the other. After
this I lay very still, fearful that I had undone all the good
of my enforced inactivity and that my rib was worse than
ever. The heavy cold and the long hours in bed had left
me as weak as a sparrow. However, I planned to build up
a terrific physique in the near future. Josephine McClinton was usually around cheering me on while I was beating up the Lynchites and in a way this always spoiled it
because a change came o'er the spirit of my dream as it
were, and Josephine and I used to end up being very
naughty indeed, which left me miserable and contrite in
spite of Herbert's cheerful advice. According to Herbert
—oh well, there is no need to go into that.

By the time I had been at school a week and nothing
desperate had happened, I perked up a lot but I still stayed
within sight of the class-room windows at play intervals
and, after school, I refrained from wandering down back
streets. At the end of the week, on Saturday afternoon, I
had the privilege of meeting Chester Montgomery. I had
already glimpsed him in the distance riding the bicycle
which had a triangular notice fixed under the bar, bearing
the legend "A. C. Wilson, Family Merchant". I had soon
gleaned that Prudence and he had made each other's
acquaintance at the back door of her employers', the
Quins', house.

Prudence had Saturday afternoon off and she arrived
at home with her bel ami in tow just a few minutes before
Les and I departed to view the final episode of "The King
of Diamonds". For the record, the character who sat behind a desk in a hood and pulled a lever, which opened a
trapdoor in the floor, turned out to be the disinherited
brother of Baron Duffelgeim. I do not think I have yet
stood in front of a desk, being interviewed, without an

uneasy feeling I might suddenly find myself precipitated down into a pit full of crocodiles. Maybe this deep-seated unease of mine was noticeable and prejudiced my interviewers, because I certainly have stood in front of a lot of desks in my time without being conspicuously victorious.

Les had been maybe a teeny bit prejudiced, too, when he described Chester Montgomery, but in the main outline he was fairly near the mark. He was no Fatty Arbuckle or Billy Bunter, or anything like that, but he was no ballet dancer either, especially viewed from the rear. I will not go so far as to say he had a squeaky voice, but it was high-pitched to emanate from a bloke's vocal box. He was fairly tall and he did have curly hair, sure enough, which bore out what Prudence had said, but I had to give in that Les was just as correct when he said maybe Chester Montgomery was the politest guy in the world. As far as I was concerned there was no maybe about it. I failed to see how anyone could be more polite without committing suicide in case they were breathing someone else's air. Chester Montgomery would have sooner fallen off a wobbling bicycle than not wave to somebody on the footpath. He was that sort of person.

When Les and I left for the flicks, Chester was already chopping wood for Ma and saying over his shoulder between chops, "No, no, Mrs Poindexter, I'll pick it up, Mrs Poindexter. I'll pick it up, Mrs Poindexter." Bang, bang. "I'll bring it all in, you just wait there, Mrs Poindexter, in case"—bang—"there's any of those chips get to flying around. Nice little tommyhawk you've got here, Mrs Poindexter." Bang, bang. "Whoops. No, I'm all right, thank you very much, only a bit of a cut, Mrs Poindexter." Bang, bang. "Oops-a-daisy, only a bit of skin, ha, ha. Soon have the old fire going now, Mrs Poindexter. Any time you want any wood cut, Mrs Poindexter. Any time."

Les opened the gate for me and bowed, but I waved him through. He waved me through. We both bowed.

Then we got stuck going through together, so we had to try again. We kept on doing this until we felt we had diverted Prudence's attention to us. She was standing on our broken-down L-shaped veranda proudly watching Chester Montgomery wielding the tommyhawk but, in the end, she could not ignore what Les and I were doing any longer. About the fourth or fifth time we got stuck in the gateway she let fly with a hunk of coal and we took off down Smythe Street laughing our fool heads off. The really funny part was that no one ever used the gate anyway, on account of nearly all the fence being down.

Chapter Ten

"A VERY NICE and obliging young man," Ma said to me one evening, apropos Chester Montgomery. "Don't yuh scoff like that about him, Eddy, as there are things yuh should know such as 'Manners maketh the man'. Not that I won't allow he is a trifle on the palavery side and a bit addicted to over-use of one's name, but all the same it is a change and a relief to have a man around who is polite enough to treat a lady *like* a lady and not sit guzzling booze, or snoring, while she chops wood and carries water, and never turn a hair, or do a hand's turn like one or two I could name offhand, yeruncle, Mister Athol Claude Cudby, springing to muh mind at this junchuh."

"Please, Natalie," said Uncle Athol, who had made an unsteady entrance a sentence or so back. "Not in front of guests, Natalie, no never. Not in front of Mr Dabney, Natalie, surely."

Ma looked out the door angrily, but a little anxiously as well, because she was sensitive about being overheard doing her block by visitors, especially anyone as important as the local undertaker. There was no one to be seen, but just then the chain pulled in the washhouse and in a moment Mr Dabney emerged doing up his fly. He soon gave up such a complicated task and took out his gold watch to consult it instead.

"Nothing but booze, booze, booze," hissed Ma. "A man

in his position, inebriated. Disgraceful. With his fly undone. Disgusting. A mortician with a gold watch and a business and nothing but a wretched slave to the bottle."

"Sssh," said Uncle Athol. "I have news for you my dear, good news." He tailed off as the chain crashed again, abortively this time, and there appeared a very tall, very thin, sallow individual with deep lines around his mouth and black hair switched back over his balding head. This newcomer was dressed in a two-piece, pin-striped suit of some dark material going green with age, and a soiled white shirt held together at the throat by as natty a little black bow tie as one might ever wish to behold. I emitted a gasp of surprise as I realized this apparition to be no other than the sinister and scarecrow-like figure I had first glimpsed at the Te Rotiha cross-roads.

Charlie Dabney was swaying to and fro on his tubby legs and holding up his gold watch at all angles to squint at it, but to the lanky and cadaverous stranger it was but the work of a moment to read the dial and acquaint the owner of the timepiece with the hour of day. For this service he was rewarded with a large cigar, a replica of the unlighted one being chewed by Charlie himself.

"A dear ole friend of Mr Dabney's, Natalie," Uncle Athol explained nervously and quickly as the visitors approached.

"Right on tea-time," hissed Ma. "You and yuh stew bums."

"Great Scott, what a wonderful woman," proclaimed Charlie Dabney. "What a won-der-ful woman. A ministering angel thou. Imagine ole Daniel Herbert cornering a gem of purest ray serene I mean to say, what, what, and ole Charlie still on the shelf, but I'll tell you something, people—"

"Are dying to meetcha, Charlie," said Uncle Athol. Uncle Athol now looked suitably apologetic at having stolen Charlie Dabney's thunder in this way.

"True enough, true enough," said Charlie Dabney. "Customers never answer ole Charlie back. Satisfaction guaranteed. Everybody potenshul client. Wanyah to meet dear, dear, ole frien' uh mine, Mrs Dee-aitch, dear old frien' from way back when. Great Scott I'm a poet and don't know it."

"Hubert Salter," said the stranger. "De-lighted to make yer acquaintance, Mrs er?"

"My sister, Mrs Poindexter," said Uncle Athol, hastening to fill the conversational gap left by Charlie Dabney, who seemed to have fallen into a reverie. "Mr Hubert Salter."

"Feel terrible, influctuating on yer like this," said the stranger. "Very good of yer I'm sure Mrs P., hope yer forgive the influctation."

"Not at*tall*, not at*tall*," said Ma, thawing out a lot. "Quite welcome, I'm sure."

The stranger adjusted his bow tie lightly.

"Take a seat, you men," said Ma, fussing around. "Here Athol, give me a lift out with the table. We'll have Dad and Herbert home any minute. You'll be having something to eat, you men, I suppose. Take that end, Eddy."

"We bought a beer or two home, Natalie," said Uncle Athol, leaning towards Ma a little and smirking in his ingratiating way. His hands were thrust deep in his trouser pockets, the fingers twiddling with the lining. "Feel that the boys might like a quick glass before participating in yuh most excellent repast."

"Oh surely," said Ma. "Tea's as good as on the table. All day in town and then beer at home, is it? I'm sure yuh friend, Mr Salter, is hungry by now and anxious to partake of something more solid than alcohol in a raw state on an empty stomach."

The stranger, Mr Salter, fingered his bow tie lightly. "Perhaps Mrs P.," he said, "we might prevail on yer to indulge in a syrup cup with us. To be frank, I have had very little in the way of liquid refreshment, being as I am only a society drinker. I do feel, however, the occasion calls for a glass. With yer permission, of course, and only if yer will condescend to accompany us."

He touched the end of his tie with the tips of his fingers as if he were lifting a rare butterfly off an even rarer orchid. Ma looked at his bow tie, greatly impressed.

"Well," she said, "I s'pose—"

Uncle Athol stumbled in with a bag holding half a dozen bottles of beer and dived out again to bring in two flagons of draught ale, by which time the tall stranger had procured a chair for Ma and prevailed on her to seat herself at the head of the table. He lowered her into the chair, gently holding one of her elbows and with his free hand stroking her back soothingly. I wished Les were here to see this performance. It began to look as if Chester Montgomery was only a novice.

"Take a seat, Mr Dabney," I cried, taking the mortician by the arm, for he had begun to rock gently to and fro.

"What, what," said Charlie emerging from his brief perpendicular encounter with Mr Sandman. "Great Scott. Wazzat? Beer! Great Scott, the lights won't go out all night."

Pop and Herbert were late rolling home in the old Dennis and, by this time, they had missed a great deal. I ducked out to meet them. The tray of the Dennis was loaded down with junk, as far as I could tell in the early darkness, so it looked like a good haul. There had been the very devil of a rumpus about Herbert not having ever had a job and the upshot had been he agreed to go out with Pop that afternoon. Standing in the feeble glimmer of the headlamps while he guided Pop to steer the Dennis through the junk, Herbert looked as disillusioned as a stadium mouse.

"Pop, Herbert," I gabbled, "yuh better come along in and see if we can get this man to do it again. He's a friend of Mr Dabney's, but acherly he's Salter the Sensational. He's toured the world hundreds of times. I tell yuh he's got a bow tie and everything. Wait till yuh see this."

They both looked so sour and sceptical, I lost patience with them and scuttled back indoors again. Just let 'em wait and see, I thought. Sure enough, I had missed out on another act. Everybody around the table looked flushed and astounded and hysterical, except Salter the Sensational, who was modestly pouring himself some refreshment.

"Whadud'e do? Whadud'e do?" I breathed at Ma across the table. She shook her head wordlessly. The stranger put his glass down and put a big, brown, sinewy paw on top of Ma's hand on the table. With his other hand he touched his bow tie lightly.

"Yer see, Mrs P.," he said, "there are more things in heaven and earth than are dreamed of in yer philosophical, Horatius. More things, Mrs P., more things." His voice sank mysteriously. "Many, many, more things."

The way he said it, made me feel the lights were getting dimmer. This guy was really something. Wait until I told Les about this. No one would believe me, I suppose. Just like Pop and Herbert, the ignorant yokels. They came in just then and even the sight of the beer did not seem to cheer Pop up much.

"Here's Pop, Mr Dabney," I said.

"Great Scott," mumbled Charlie. "Dee-aitch where yuh been? Who's dead, yuh old scoundrel? Got to keep yuh ear to the ground to make a pound."

"Danyel," Ma was trying to get a word in. "This is your turn to wait for yuh tea. I want yuh to meet Mr Sensational Salter, who has toured the world times without number and performed his feats in places which to the like of us are merely something out of the Arabia Nights. My husband—Mr Salter."

The wizard, for such without doubt he was, arose with

alacrity and, so great was his height, reached clean across the table to shake hands with Pop. Herbert, the clot, had vanished.

"Yer must join us in a syrup cup," said Salter the Sensational. "Yer are a dealer, sir, I believe." Quick as a flash he touched his bow tie.

"Thank you. Thank you," said Pop, managing to tear his eyes off the bow tie. "That is correct, Mr Salter. Thank you, a glass of ale will be extremely acceptable." Glug, glug. "Possibly I could request yuh to replenish the goblet. You are correct. I am a dealer of long standing in the locality. A dealer, sir, in antiques."

I guess he was right at that. I was unable to contain myself longer. "Do the one with the teapot. Show us the India-rubber man trick, Mr Salter. That's the best of the lot—"

Salter held up his hand. The others laughed at my youthful enthusiasm. Pop put his hand on top of my head.

"For yer father, son," said the mysterious visitor, "I will perform an amazing and dangerous act of skill and daring seldom, if ever, witnesseth beyond the confines of the *mistykeist*."

I may as well confess that for a long time, years in fact, I did not wake up that he was saying "mystic East". They were favourite words of his, but he brought them out, after a pause, in such a sudden way that they sounded like one strange, outlandish word beyond our ken.

The enthralled hush as Salter the Sensational took up a position in front of the fireplace flushed a still sulking Herbert out of the bedroom. Now he was going to see something!

Slowly, our eyes riveted on him, the tall, gaunt man slipped his hand beneath the lapel of his coat. Dead silence.

The door opened to admit Prudence. She looked around the kitchen in astonishment.

"What cooks?" she said, and well she might have asked.

"Ma," she resumed, obviously assuming we were all a bit loofy, and disregarding us accordingly, "Chester has asked me to go to the Film Society Club evening with him. It's a Charlie Chaplin and it's a real old beaut, he tells me. We get supper up at the rooms and I've had some fish and chips, so I'll just go out without any tea, eh, Ma? O.K.? Chester's calling for me just after eight."

No one said a word because Salter the Sensational had withdrawn his hand from beneath his coat and was pointing straight across the room at Prudence.

"So," he said.

"So what?" said Prudence.

"Pru," said Ma, feebly.

"So," said Salter. There ensued a long silence and then he beckoned her mildly.

"Come over here, mer dear." Prudence did not say anything, but she went slowly across to where the stranger was standing. She looked puzzled. Then she stopped dead with her hands on her hips and her feet apart and the bang of hair in one eye as if to say, "I'll be damned if I'll go any further."

Actually she said, "Yeah."

I had known for a long time she had been busy knitting a frock for herself. Tonight, I realized, she was wearing it, but I did not think it made her look as pretty as usual. The shade of wool was unkind to her complexion, but the frock itself, without doubt, did things for her figure. It was skin-tight for one thing and gave one's imagination a back wind and downhill slope.

Prudence was looking up at the tall man by the mantelpiece and from where I was sitting it looked like a staring-out contest. Salter the Sensational gave his bow tie a gossamer flick.

"Behold," he said, producing from under his coat the longest-bladed knife I have ever seen. It must be remembered this is some time ago, but I am prepared to swear

107

it had a blade nearly a foot long. It caught the light like a mirror. Prudence started to scream, but he was still holding her eye and the scream faded to a gasp. We all gasped. I had my back to Herbert, but my guess is that he gasped too. Probably Herbert's gasp was the biggest gasp of the lot, would be my guess.

Slowly Salter the Sensational arched over backwards, standing flat-foot and holding the hilt of the knife by a finger and thumb. Under our hypnotized and appalled gaze he lowered that impossible, glittering length of blade down his throat until his thumb touched his lower lip. It would have been possible to stick a scythe down Ma's throat, her mouth was open so wide. Prudence spun around towards me with her hands covering her eyes. Over her hair, which tickled my nose, I saw the great man withdraw and triumphantly spin the knife, clean and shiningly bloodless. He looked down in disappointment at Prudence's turned back. His nose was huge, veined, pockmarked. I avoided looking at his nose. It was a spectacle I felt no desire to contemplate for a long period.

"Great Scott," said Charlie Dabney. "At this rate the lights won't go out all night." Now it was his turn to put his hand under his coat and produce something. He placed the bottle on the table and it caught the light in the same way the big knife had.

"This is my turn," Uncle Athol suddenly piped. "I'll swallow that." He cackled like an imbecile, but I looked at him with a certain admiration.

Prudence seemed to be settling down on my chest for the night. I put my arms around her. Then we heard the crash. Herbert had apparently been slowly sliding down the door jamb of our bedroom in a dead faint and had just done the last lap in a gallop. Prudence was the last to realize what had happened, not counting Mr Dabney.

"Where's that man?" she whispered to me. I was looking over my shoulder at the soles of my brother's boots.

We pulled them off and got him into bed. A suck at Mr Dabney's recently produced bottle helped Herbert to co-operate with us.

"Over my dead body," protested Charlie Dabney when, acting on Ma's instructions, I grabbed the bottle from under his nose. "Over my dead body. Great Scott, what'm I saying? *My* dead body. Who's gunna foot the bill, thas what I wanna know. *My* dead body!"

"And this is what comes about of playing ducks and drakes with the appointed and proper time for nourishment," cried Ma. "This is a judgment on all of us for sitting about, taking alcohol in a raw state on an empty stomach, while the poor boy stood there faint with hunger, watching people swallowing swords in front of his own fireplace, after a day of toil and nothing but a burnt chop for lunch.

"To a great degree, I blame muh own brother for this cally-amity," continued Ma, "muh own brother, Athol Cudby, who for many years has styled himself as muh husband's partner and accomplice genrilly speaking and yet, on account of his rupchuh, has been of no practical assistance to the firm of Dee-aitch Poindexter. Many's the time when muh husband has fallen into bed exhausted from his labours and with muh own eyes I have seen muh own brother—yes it's true, Athol, so shut yuh trap—muh own brother, as bright as a button, sally forth to spend what has been earned by the sweat of muh husband's brow, in riotous living and raw alcohol until the crack uv dawn. And a fat lot you care, Athol Cudby, if now muh own son has fainted dead away from a strained heart and the shock of watching people yuh have brought into the house from the hotel at tea-time, swallowing swords right and left in front of his own fireplace."

"It may interest yuh to know, my dear Natalie," said Uncle Athol, who always appeared to be looking at someone else on account of his bung eye, "that I have this very day accepted employment with my dear friend, Mr Dabney. Mr Dabney has kindly offered me a position in the old-established firm of Dabney and Son, undertakers of taste and distinction."

"Calls for a drink, calls for a drink," exclaimed old Charlie. "Pass your glass to Charlie, thou good and faithful servant."

"Pychah," snorted Ma.

"Right-hand man, absholooly. Regards, regards."

"Regards, Charlie."

Charlie Dabney now leaned back and, holding up both hands, palms outwards, began to clench and unclench his fingers rhythmically.

"What in the name of God Almighty are you supposed to be doing now?" demanded Ma, hands on hips, as Uncle Athol started to do the very same thing.

"Neon sign," explained Uncle Athol in an embarrassed aside. "Charlie's getting one of these here new-fangled neon signs."

"Brainwave, brainwave," said Charlie, opening and shutting his hands. "*Cremations arranged. Cremation arrainsh.*"

"*Cremations arrainsh,*" chanted Uncle Athol, opening and shutting his hands. "*Cremations arrainsh.*"

"Well now I am convinced beyond all doubt that I'm living in a bloody nuthouse," stormed Ma.

I looked to see whether Salter the Sensational thought so too, but he was draped over the mantelpiece and Prudence was looking up at him, fascinated, and holding out her hand. The lines around the wizard's mouth were almost gullies, they were so deep. I had observed before that the deepening of those lines was the great man's way of smiling. Slowly he withdrew the fearsome knife again and passed it to Prudence. She fingered the steel in awe. He retrieved it from her, but instead of returning it to its place of concealment under his coat, he pressed the hilt lightly against Prudence's chin so that the blade glittered down between her breasts, reaching to the pit of her stomach.

"Behold, my child," said Salter, "its length. Behold how far that razor-sharp edge would sink into yer lush and virginal body."

There was no disputing that this Salter was the real McCoy and it was without any doubt a great honour and a marvellous stroke of luck to have him under our roof all to ourselves; but right then I entertained a creepy feeling. Even if he had toured the world times without number, I felt convinced that there was something screwy about him.

Now he was balancing the knife on the palm of his hand, tip pointing at the roof. His eyes were glittering. Doggone it there *was* something screwy about him. As he lowered his head slowly floorwards his eyelids began to droop, hooding the crazy gleam I had glimpsed. Fascinated, Prudence's eyes followed the descending tip of steel. The knife was trembling slightly and the light winked its way up and down the blade like a diamond. Salter now steadied the tip of the knife with his other hand and turned the edge a little so the light shone directly on Prudence's staring eyes.

"Watch the lights dancing," he said softly. "The dancing lights. The lights dancing. Dancing and dreaming. See how they dance and dream, mer darling." One of his eyes, just in one corner, moved and took me in, standing close to them and I felt this man's hatred for my presence come out of him like a wave. And now I hated him too. Hated and feared him.

"The dreaming lights," he whispered.

To do what I did, I had to remind myself that this was our own kitchen, that Ma was in the pantry, that Pop, Uncle Athol and Charlie Dabney were guzzling grog at the table just behind me; but I did it, and I am glad and proud. I coughed, and the evil spell he was weaving shattered like a dropped electric light bulb. Prudence turned her head towards me. She looked bewildered.

"Wait, wait," said Salter urgently. The sweat was pouring out of him now, glistening on his big, jutting beak of a nose. The corner of an eye that he spared for me twitched in my direction again, and again I felt the wave of hatred for me he exuded. It was as real as an octopus squirting its inky fluid.

"Wait, wait," he repeated. He laid the knife flat against Prudence, this time with the hilt down against her stomach, the contour of which was so plainly etched against her knitted frock that I could almost see the fish and chips. Now the blade pointed upwards between her breasts. "See, see," he said. "See how long it is, mer dear, and how far up into yer lovely young body it reaches."

One thing I could see anyway and that was, holding the hilt of the knife against her stomach the way he was, he had the tips of his fingers pressing hard up between her legs. Prudence turned away from him with a jerk as if she were only just capable of wrenching herself free from his spell. Feet apart, she stood still between Salter and me. Her hair had fallen over one eye again. Salter gave me a cold, evil look. His eyes lost their gleam and became muddled and murky as he looked at me. I wondered how drunk he was. He put the knife away and I glimpsed a long sheath under his armpit. He ran the sleeve of his coat quickly across his sweat-drenched face. As he did this, one end of the bow tie came loose from his collar and hung down on his dirty shirt-front like a dead beetle. His elbow had caught the bow tie and snapped the ancient ribbon. Now, instead of being impressive, the bow tie only looked absurd. It was a slender thread for a complete aura of mastery and mystery to hang by, and it had snapped. I am unable to say whether it was seeing the bow tie hanging like that, or whether it was just the abrupt easing of tension, but suddenly Prudence laughed her high-pitched, girlish laugh. There could be no mistaking the fact that she was laughing at Salter. It was very rude of her, but next thing I realized I was laughing at Salter too. The two of us stood looking up at the gaunt, lined, evil face with its great nose and we laughed and laughed.

Salter stared at us uncomprehendingly, despairingly, and then suddenly his hand flew to his throat. Our laughter died away. His face worked as if he were in pain. He tore the tie away from his neck savagely, so savagely the top button of his dirty white shirt popped off and fell to the floor at his feet. He held the tie swallowed up by his clenched fist in front of him. I had never seen anyone so blind and shaking with anger. I had seen people go white and sometimes red with anger, but never black, really black. Prudence and I were frozen. His blood was black! The blood of Salter the Sensational could turn black. He walked with great, slow, unsteady strides across the room to the door. He opened the door and then wheeled around to face the room again. His mouth was dragged down like a bloodhound's. A clawlike hand reached over the unsuspecting and nodding head of Charlie Dabney and seized the bottle of Hennessey's Three Star Brandy. For a lingering, menacing second his gaze sought us out and then he was gone.

Prudence looked at me wide-eyed. There was a lot of talk and expostulating going on around the kitchen table, but Prudence and I were in a little sound-proofed compartment of our own.

"We shouldn't have laughed," Pru whispered. "I'm frightened now, Neddy. We shouldn't have laughed at him."

"Where's my brandy?" Charlie Dabney was demanding querulously. "Where's my brandy gone? What scoundrel decamped with my bottle of Hennessey's Three Star Brandy?"

Then we heard the heavy footsteps coming up the steps. The loose board creaked. Thinking of Salter, his great height, the vulture-like face, the strange eyes and the long knife, Prudence and I clung to each other in terror. Prudence turned away and stumbled over to the mantelpiece with a giant sigh, her relief was so great when the doorway framed the fat figure and inane, ingratiating smile of Chester Montgomery.

Chapter Eleven

AFTER EASTER we began to count the days to the May holidays.

The new serial was called "The Fire God's Treasure" and it was turning out better than we expected, although I still preferred ambushes with tommyguns to drama on jungle trails, rakish touring cars to pith helmets.

Len Ramsbottom, I was now forced to admit, was a better typist than he had appeared to be while taking our statements. He could still head Prudence off and she was getting pretty slick.

Uncle Athol had a job driving the hearse. Presumably he had other duties, but what they could be had me beaten.

Herbert went out with Pop in the Dennis by day and marked in the pool-room in the evening.

Josephine McClinton was wearing longer frocks, the meanie.

Les did not really believe me about Salter the Sensational, but he entered into the spirit of it and we tried it out with the kitchen knife. We tried to make things disappear by waving our arms around and saying *"mistykeist"*, but the spell neglected to work.

We stole a bottle of applejack from a drunken woman sitting in the gutter and we took it to Fitzherbert's shed. We drank it and sang and fell over and then we tried out what the Lynchites must be doing with Peachy, but it did not work either. We didn't try saying *"mistykeist"*. We never admitted even vaguely remembering the episode again. I guess we were pretty ashamed all right.

We were so ashamed that we will never mention what happened in the shed that gloomy afternoon as long as we live. I was worse than Les that day. My legs were heavy and my head spun. When I reached home I was sick with desire for a girl. In my bedroom, thinking feverishly about Josephine McClinton and heaven knows how many other girls and even grown women I had seen about the town, a sudden twist in my applejack-clouded mental processes set me shaking all over. Ousting every favourite erotic image from my mind was now the vivid picture of Prudence, in her tight and skimpy black knickers, swinging from the beam in the twilit, musky-smelling shed. I was obsessed with the recollection of her legs and the coppery glow beneath the soft skin. I shook from head to toe with a delicious desire. I was powerless in the grip of that desire. I hung around the washhouse waiting for Prudence, listening, above my hammering blood, for her footfalls, and planning for her to catch me exposed, so that her blood would race as mysteriously as mine. What Prudence actually did see when at last she came was her worthless brother vomiting his vile applejack-soaked heart down the W.C.

"Crikey," she said. "You, too. Don't tell me yuh bin on the booze too like Pop and Uncle Athol. Don't tell me that, Eddy."

After Easter the weather was colder and the house damper. When the fire went out in the kitchen the only place to be was in bed with the blankets pulled up.

The golden nuts on the karaka-tree were beginning to shrivel and fall. They were all over the narrow footpath along Smythe Street and out on the road too.

We put a lot of tins up on top of the ceiling to catch the leaks.

116

For three blissful days I was a dog owner. It was the skinniest, most miserable, all-night-long-yelpingest, face-lickingest creature that ever limped into Klynham from God knows where, but I loved every scraggy, fleabitten inch of it. Ma and Prudence pointed the finger of scorn and complained bitterly, but behind my back they fed it like cannibals with a missionary. One grey dawn it limped on its way again and left me desolate.

About the time I had the dog I was thoroughly wretched, but I recall that period of my boyhood with tenderness. Suddenly, overnight it seemed, I had become ashamed of our tumbledown house with its broken windows, littered yard, and collapsed fence; ashamed of Uncle Athol, ashamed of Pop going around making himself a laughing-stock by calling himself things like "valuer" and "antique dealer" when, all the time, everyone knew he was only a boozy junk collector. Maybe he did draw the line at bones, but did that make him a "valuer" or "antique dealer"? Les Wilson was lucky having a merchant for a father. I would have died, I think, if he had told me he was going to join the dancing class Josephine McClinton attended, but the idea never crossed his head. I had found out that quite a few of my contemporaries were attending this dancing class. It was held upstairs over a garage (a firm which finally headed Charlie Dabney off to getting the first neon sign in Klynham) and I used to slink past at night and hear the stamp of feet doing a palais glide to "Ten Pretty Girls", or a foxtrot to "Roll Along Covered Wagon, Roll Along". This was the greatest piece of music ever written, I believed, in addition to being the only one I could whistle, and down in the dark street listening to that happy, secret world, I thought my heart would burst. "Anyway, you love me, don't yuh, ole pal?" I said to the dog. "Yuh don't care if I'm a Poindexter, do yuh, old pal? and I'll tell yuh this, pup, in these parts the Poindexters are just so much riff-raff."

117

Sometimes I think I walked the legs off my dog and that is the reason it cleared out. I fail to see why it should have found the going too tough as my feet were bare too and it had four to my two, well, three counting out the gimpy one. Perhaps my bitter reflections acted as fuel and the dog did not have anything of that nature to fall back on. I must have walked hundreds of miles. A love for a place that one can never lose can strike up through the soles of one's bare feet, I am sure. No matter how unhappy one may be, the love for the earth itself fairly soaks up through the soles of a person's bare feet until it reaches the heart. Around and about the weed-pierced footpaths of every back street we padded, generally ending up for a short spell under a certain macrocarpa-tree from whence it was possible to discern the glimmering white outline of the McClinton residence nestling in the heart of a well-attended shrubbery. Some nights I even set out along the beach road, as it was called, a quite erroneous name because there was no beach but only great, precipitous cliffs and, anyway, the road petered out into the sandhills miles before that. Out here the wind soughed in the wires and I could hear the sea, and this elemental atmosphere suited my mood. Out here the only lights were lanterns in Maori whares, set away back in the sandhills among the acres of lupin and the kumara gardens.

After Easter and the first deep frosts, the days were clear and cold as a mountain stream, and the distant scream of the big saw at the mill became a part of our lives. Otherwise the town dreamed on in silence. The clouds were acoustic tiles. When a train shuffled through, its whistle was the howl of a blues trumpet.

Uncle Athol told us for the five-hundredth time he was going to borrow a hammer and nails and fix the loose board on the veranda before someone broke their neck.

Pop said he found a new battery for the Dennis at the rubbish tip, but I saw an advertisement in the paper for a battery that had been left at the bus depot and had been taken by mistake, the ad. hinted politely. I saw Pop reading the paper and then he went out with it to the washhouse. I was beginning to have my doubts about Pop.

But I loved Ma. One afternoon I found Ma sitting in Prudence's room. She was sitting on the floor. The wallpaper was hanging down on three of the walls and when I say hanging down I mean really hanging down, in great, mouldy folds. I went in because I thought I had heard a sound, and it was Ma crying. She was sitting on the bare floor, crying.

"The poor girl, Eddy," she said. "Oh, the poor girl. Just look at it."

I went and sat on the floor too and that was the closest we had ever been, I guess, since she breast-fed me. It was a rainy, dark afternoon. We sat on the bare floor without speaking for some time. I felt older after that.

I started the worrying habit after that too. This was a real bad habit to get into. (Uncle Athol did not believe in worrying about anything. He was dead against worry. "Why worry?" he used to say. "Why worry and get thin legs?")

Now I knew why Prudence kept her door shut and the curtains across the window. She was ashamed. She had not used to care. Working in a wealthy home like Quin's had opened her eyes, I suppose; but she never complained or anything like that. One day I sneaked into her room and she had hung a little picture on the one intact wall. I saw her few possessions on the worm-eaten dressing-table. I could have sat down and howled myself.

Prudence may not have had a bedroom like Josephine McClinton had—not that I have ever seen Josephine's or was ever likely to—but one thing was for sure, she had admirers. A little chap in a college blazer, who threw his head back when he laughed, had joined the line-up by this time. It turned out he was the pride and hope of the

Quins. This must have been getting near the May holidays. The school Tony Quin attended broke up for vacation earlier than our plebeian institution. Except for Len Ramsbottom and, of course, old Les, all Prudence's conquests seemed to be made at Quin's place and, except for young Tony Quin himself, made on the back doorstep. It was there that Chester Montgomery had lost his heart; it was there Cupid's dart connected amidships with the butcher boy (what a goof) and on the same hallowed spot the representative of Waller's Household Remedies and the ditto of the Climax Insurance Company went head over heels. The household remedy man had a bald spot and the insurance man a toothbrush moustache. Les reckoned the insurance man used to bite his nails and then give them a quick scrub in the brisk little moustache. Les was becoming embittered. He had found and wore a pith helmet (well, most of a pith helmet) like the hero of "The Fire God's Treasure", but he was still cutting no ice with Prudence.

On Sunday mornings, about 10.30, there were always a few people getting out of cars and standing in groups outside the Temple of the Brethren of the Lamb, which is opposite our place but facing Winchester Street. There was a Hammond organ in the Temple and whoever played it was a marvellous musician. I nearly used to break down when I heard those thrilling tones. I do not know who played that organ, but they were wasting their time in Klynham. They could have toured the world like Salter the Sensational. The music used to give me goose pimples and make me more determined than ever to reform and never imagine Josephine McClinton lying in the lucerne hay, full of applejack with her pants off, ever again. It was a little quicker to cut down Winchester Street to get to the town from our place but lately, Sunday mornings, I had got into the habit of using Smythe Street, so that I would not hear the Hammond organ, it upset me so.

I forgot this particular Sunday and I was heading around the corner of the Temple of the Brethren of the Lamb when I saw a group of people who were so far gone that the strains of the organ meant nothing to them. They would not have heard it if it had started playing "Hold That Tiger". They were standing across the street outside the Sorrensons' higgledy-piggledy picket fence, eight of them, not counting two diminutive, sexless, finger-sucking, little upstarts wearing only singlets. Jim Sorrenson had married a girl with Maori blood in her, almost white herself, but she had borne children the same military-tan shade as Dr Mahoney's shoes.

I could not believe it was Prudence in the centre of the group because she looked such a hussy. She was wearing a dress she would have had trouble getting into when she was ten years old and would not have been in now if it had not been split up the side like a sausage dumped in hot fat. My own sister, and I had to find out in the street she had hair under her arms. That is the sort of sleeveless jumper she was wearing over that old dress. Out in the street, across the road from the Temple of the Brethren of the Lamb! With the organ playing! It was almost too much. The organ played one of those soft, quivering chords and I could feel my eyelids flickering and my eyeballs receding as I tried to cope.

The whole lot of them were around her, even Len Ramsbottom, who was on duty and wearing a helmet and everything. The butcher boy was there without his blue apron, but it was impossible to mistake him with those bumps on his forehead and the way he kept jumping up in the air and slapping his knees together. Chester Montgomery was there hanging on to everybody's word and occasionally scratching his behind. Among those present was that little squirt, Tony Quin, with his hands in his college blazer, laughing and throwing his head back regular as clockwork, the Waller's Household Remedy man

121

whose van was parked handy, and the insurance bloke who was talking nineteen to the dozen. He gave Prudence a cigarette and lit it for her. There was a white open sports-car parked at the kerb. I do not know whether the car belonged to Tony Quin or the insurance bloke. It was hardly the sort of car to be owned by a Brethren of the Lamb, not with the exhaust hoses sweeping back outside the bonnet. Last of all I saw poor Angela Potroz leaning up against the lamp-post and smiling as was her wont, but obviously jealous and miserable.

Prudence kept on putting a hand on one hip, waggling herself around, and tossing the bang of hair out of her eye. The butcher boy was jumping higher all the time and I could hear his knees bang together in mid-air, even from where I was across the street. The insurance bloke was still holding forth and eloquence must have won the day because Prudence made a sudden dash for the sports-car. Showing off as was to be expected, he did not open his cutaway door, but just jumped over behind the wheel. Prudence swung her legs over too and my eyelids went on the flicker again.

The motor snarled into action. I heard Prudence yell out to the others "C'mon, c'mon." It was only a two-seater, so the slow reaction of her audience is understandable. I have to hand it to young Quin. He landed on the boat-tail of the machine as it moved away and scrambled to safety on the shoulders of the occupants, his arms around both their necks. They departed with an exhaust blast that nearly blew Constable Ramsbottom's helmet off.

By three o'clock that afternoon they were still not home. Angela Potroz and I were bound together by a common loyalty in silence. We told Ma that Prudence had gone for a drive with the insurance bloke, whose name, Norman Bryant, Angela surprisingly supplied; but of the mad circumstances and the type of car we said nothing.

I was only superficially worried about Prudence, to

whose complete downfall I was now resigned, but I was very anxious to steer Angela off somewhere and try out kissing her. The trouble with Angela was that she was such a sweet-natured girl, forever volunteering to run messages for everybody and forever combing the kids' hair, even backing me into a corner and having a lash at my cowslick. She was not the sort of person you envisaged having any trouble kissing once you could corner her.

A few minutes after four Constable Ramsbottom put in an appearance with his portable typewriter under his arm. He took a much dimmer view of Prudence's absence than any of us had. He took me aside and somehow or other Angela came too.

"Fa-har be it from me to hinterfere," he said, "and fa-har be it from me to cause your mother unnecessary wo-horry, but Oi feel that under the soikumstances inquiries should be hinstigated."

I concurred listlessly. I would not have imagined there was room for Angela and me as well as the policeman in his tiny Austin seven, but we managed. He put us in the back seat. From there his shoulders looked incredibly broad. He had not driven more than a few hundred yards when we saw the butcher boy, Herman, standing on a corner. I never found out if he had another name, or whether that was his Christian or surname.

"There's Herman," cried Angela, and the Austin squeaked to a halt. When Herman saw Angela waving at him from the little car he leapt about three feet into the air and banged his knees together with a loud clonk. He shambled across the road to us wearing a vacuous smile which the sight of the driver distorted without vanquishing. No, he had no idea where Prudence was. I watched him through the back window as we drove off. He stood in the middle of the road gaping after us. He stood perfectly still, but I continued to keep him under observation as we got further away. I was determined to keep my eyes on him until he was out of sight. Just as we rounded a long bend, which finally cut off my rear view, I got my reward. I distinctly saw him rising up in the air. I turned around with a sigh.

Being driven around your own town in the back seat of a cop's car is not like seeing the sights in a neighbour's car, or jogging around in your own car. The whole town looks different. People look different. I saw Les Wilson walking along and he stared straight at the little car, but, although I nearly banged my head through the celluloid side curtain, he looked away without seeing me. As we jolted and creaked across the main street I saw Salter the Sensational leaning against the wall of the Federal Hotel. He looked about seven feet tall. He had the green suit on, but he was holding his coat together at the throat so I am unable to say about the bow tie. I shivered. Angela said "What's wrong?"

I said "That man, I'll tell you about him after."

"What man?" said Angela. I looked, but Salter had disappeared.

"*Mistykeist*," I muttered. "Oh nothing, Angela. I'll tell you after."

We parked outside the Hillview private boardinghouse, a big two-storied place with tennis courts.

"Oi do not perceive the racing vehicle," remarked Constable Ramsbottom. Apparently he knew all about the insurance agent, where he was domiciled and everything. Apparently he knew all about the Waller's Home Remedy man too, because the next stop was the Jubilee Hotel, an establishment which had had its liquor licence taken off it and was now just a cheap accommodation house, a flop. The Waller firm van was parked outside, but Constable Ramsbottom emerged from the Jubilee without having accomplished anything, a fact obvious by the conversation of the garrulous old dame who accompanied him as far as the door.

"Tony Quin," I suggested to him, as he squeezed through the driver's door.

"Yus," said our stalwart chauffeur. "However, Oi am disinclined to approach the Quin family until Oi have more hinformation. Perhaps yourself, or Miss Potroz—?"

"Sure," we concurred.

So this was where Prudence worked. The large, white house appeared to be empty.

Angela and I prowled around the velvet lawns and the scrubbed verandas knocking on doors and French windows until we were suddenly confronted by a character who looked like an aged Bertie Wooster. His mouth hung open, and when he had finally told us what we wanted to know —information liberally punctuated with "gads" and "what what's"—it fell open again as if the most amazing point of the whole conversation was that he had taken any part in it. He was wearing a smoking jacket and a cravat.

I was shaking my head at Len Ramsbottom and trying to open the back door of the Austin for Angela when the white sports-job roared up and stopped. Tony Quin ran across the road, nodded at us and went up the path into the grounds of his house. Prudence came across the road much more slowly. The motor was still running in the white roadster and, behind the steering wheel, toothbrush moustache was staring straight ahead.

Len Ramsbottom emerged from the Austin; and Prudence, who was going to speak to me and Angela, stopped dead. Now she really did have a dirty face and her hair was windblown into a wild disarray which, in Prudence's case, only enhanced her beauty. When she stood still in the middle of the lane looking surprised and dismayed, the wind, which, although gentle enough, had a real bite in it, whipped her thin, inadequate dress back between her glowing legs. It was the wind local jesters spoke of as the "lazy" wind—sooner go through you than around you. Through us all it went on its ruthless way, but the army of dry leaves it shepherded, shilly-shallied reluctantly and clung to Len Ramsbottom's coat and my shirt and Angela's hair. Joyfully the fluttering leaves swooped from us to Prudence. The motor stalled in the white roadster and the smoke ceased to spurt from the exhausts. In the sudden quiet the branches of the trees, which hung over the lane on both sides, creaked and strained. Unseen in the fathomless greyness of the sky a bird sang. The starter whirred and the motor throbbed again. Under cover of this sound Prudence addressed us and it was now manifest that she was flouncing angry. I realize now that Prudence must have been a lot deeper than we had allowed for and also deeply unhappy; in fact, as miserable as hell. It grieves me to be obliged to record what she said.

"Are yuh looking fuh me?" she demanded to know. "Are yuh all out to make muh life a misery? Am I a baby, or something? Can't I take a single step without muh family and the whole police force setting out after me like a pack uv bloodhounds? Can't I even go fuh a ride in a car without being hounded down and made a fool of? So help muh God, I can't! Yud think I was a bloody criminal. Hounded down! Hounded down! Questions alla time. Where yuh been? Whatcha bin doing? You wait, Neddy Poindexter, and you too, Len Ramsbottom. Make a fool outa me, would yuh, in front of people that make me feel like I amount to something, and don't just sleep in a corner like a mangy old dog? All you wanna do is make me out a laughing-stock in front of people that make me feel I am somebody."

She glared at us and I saw her clench her fingers. It occurred to me she might be on the verge of weeping.

"Yes, SOMEBODY," she shouted above the sound of the engine. "Not just a FRIGGIN' GHOST."

The use of this frightful word on those dewy lips right out in the middle of the road put the stopper on things altogether. Len Ramsbottom wedged himself into his bug

126

of a car and, set-faced, drove off and left Angela and me standing in the gutter.

Prudence stared after the little car and it seemed to me her rage had evaporated. She looked at Angela and me and the only word I can think of to describe her glance is "imploring". Then she looked down the lane again, stuck out her tongue, and fled back to the roadster.

In the empty lane Angela and I looked at each other, big-eyed. I removed a leaf from her hair. It had been annoying me for some time.

"Just can't think what musta got into Prudence," I said. "If yuh ask me, she's gone nuts. If yuh told me she'd yell out a word like that right out in the middle uv the road, I wouldn't have believed it. If there's one word that Ma simply won't tolerate at home, it's that word Prudence yelled out right in the middle uv the road. Ma ud skin her. Ma goes crook enough if she hears Pop or Uncle Athol say that when they're boozed up, let alone Prudence. Right out in the middle of the road. Phew!"

"I dunno what you mean," complained Angela. "Prudence didn't say hello to me either. She was funny."

We set off for home. The footpath was so narrow we had to walk single file, me first.

Chapter Twelve

ONE NIGHT during the following week I was lying awake on my back in the bed by the window and I heard a locomotive, hauling freight from the hinterland to the coast, bellow thrice. I heard a short squabble between cats in the junk in the yard. I heard a hedgehog snort. I heard night-birds cry as they passed quickly on high. Soon the moon began to hurt my eyes. When I turned over on my left side I could hear my heart beating. I pressed my lips against Josephine McClinton's and the kapok of the ragged pillow tickled my nose. I arose, wheeling gracefully into the airy nothingness of sleep. The nothingness about me turned into a whirling tunnel. My astral self braced itself for the launching signal, but I was curiously drained, apathetic. Suddenly I became afraid. Afraid of sleep? No, of death! I could feel my skin tautening over my cheekbones and my blood running cold. The few cells of my brain still unnumbed began to fight like blazes. Jesus, this was no sleep; Josephine was a corpse; I was dying in her blackening arms, falling down a well forever.

These ideas are unpleasant to say the least. I will not go so far as to say I sat bolt upright, but I will allow I propped myself up on one elbow. I must have either been asleep or so close it makes no difference, because a heterogeneous collection of faces receded through the darkness at sickening velocity. I picked out a leering

Josephine McClinton among the collection of awful faces. Others I am unable to identify, mainly because most of them appeared to have been defunct for two or three million years. I must have had nerves of steel in those days because only a strangled scream escaped my lips.

When first I heard the running footsteps they seemed as if they must belong to the same nightmare. Surely no one fled pellmell down Smythe Street at this late hour. Whose fleet footsteps rang so loudly in the moon-haunted, wintry night? But they were real enough. They skidded into our yard. The board on the veranda creaked. Our back door flew open.

"Neddy, Neddy, are yuh 'wake?"

"Yeah, waz wrong?"

Prudence came in and pulled on the light. She saw the open window and jerked the light off again.

"Shut the window," she whimpered. I complied, which involved removing a flat piece of board which I employed to hold the lower sash open.

"Draw yuh curtain."

There was no curtain, but by standing up in bed I reached the bottom of the sagging, torn blind and drew it down. In the electric light Prudence looked distraught.

"Neddy," she said, "that awful man. I've never been so scared in all muh life. I nearly dropped dead uv fright and that's fuh sure."

"What man? Who?"

"Neddy," said Prudence, "Uh reckon I'm a lucky girl to be here with yuh alive right now. Uh reckon I jus' nearly had my throat cut by a bloody, great knife yuh could skin a nelephant with."

"Salter the Sensational," I said aghast. Prudence nodded and blew out a lot of air.

"Boy," she said. "Yuh not gunna find me wandering the streets at night after this. Not without a bodyguard. Even then yuh won't catch me coming along Smythe Street after dark after this, no sir. Not fuh little Prudence."

"Willyuh tell me what happened! Will you please *continue*?"

"Well," said Pru, "they asted me to stay on late at the house tonight, 'cause Mr and Mrs Quin's having a party, see. Tony was gunna bring me home, but his Ma went crook and said I'd be O.K. I was a big girl, this wasn't Port somewhere or other."

"Port Sigh-eed," I said.

"Thas right," said Prudence, bestowing on me a flicker of admiration. "Thas the place she said awright. Wherever the hell it might be. Well, looky, I get just a little way along Smythe Street and y'know that old garage where there's never a car, but only bags of cement and firewood and stuff?"

"Yeah, yeah."

"Well, I never like walkin' past there much at night, it's so dark, and I always jump off the footpath out onto the road until I get past, not that I ever really thought there ever would be anyone hiding in there, but boy—" she shuddered.

"Go on, go on," I pressed, agog.

"Well, I nearly didn't bother to jump out on the road tonight. I hate to think what ud happened if I hadn't, boy." She shuddered again. "Lucky I jumped out on the road because just as I did I saw that face."

Now it was my turn to shudder. I looked at our shadows on the torn blind.

"Listen," I said. "I'm going over to muh own bed. Herbert can sleep here tonight, I've had this."

When I had moved over to the bed against the wall, Prudence resumed. "Well, when I saw that face looking at me I nearly jumped outa muh skin I got such a norful fright."

"Where was he—in the shed?"

"Yeah, but hang on, yuh ain't heard nothin' yet. Next

thing I hear a voice sorta whisper, *Proo-oo-dence, Proo-oo-dence*, y'know that sorta soft voice, *Proo-oo-dence, Proo-oo-dence*—"

"Shut up," I said terrified. "Go on, go on."

"Well, say I was too scared to run, but I musta sorta kept on walking sideways and I see this big, long shadow coming out of the shed reaching out to me, *Proo-oo-dence, Proo-oo-dence*, and I let out one yell tuh wake the dead and took to muh scrapers. And how! Muh hair was standing on end, boy."

"Shee-whit!" I said.

"Yuh can say that again," said Prudence.

"Look here," I said. "This is worse than you think: This Salter must be laying for us because we laughed at him. Oh boy, I don't like this. Not a weird character like that with that knife."

"Maybe it's only me," said Prudence. "Maybe he's only laying for me. Maybe he's a sex-oh."

We gawked at each other.

"I don't like this so much," I said.

"Oh, I just love it," said Prudence. "I think it's just dandy having a nice man like Mr Salter waiting in a shed for me night after night with a bloody, great knife, saying, *Proo-oo-dence, Proo-oo-dence*—"

"Shut up," I hissed.

We sat for a while and then I said, "Maybe yuh better tell the police."

"An' I damn' well would too," said Prudence. "But look at what I went and did on Sunday. How can I? Gee, I've mucked things up, Neddy."

It was my private fear that Prudence had mucked things up all right, just like Winnie and Connie had, but at least they had been older and had got married. All week it had been breaking my heart, seeing Ma pottering happily around not knowing what happened on Sunday. When I thought of what was going to happen when Ma found out

Prudence was in the family way to an insurance agent with a toothbrush moustache and her only just sixteen and everything—well I just refused to let myself think about it. It did not bear thinking about. And it made me feel almost ill to think of Prudence actually knowing what "you-know" felt like. It was the first time since Sunday we had even spoken and this looked like a chance to get the inside story.

"Look, Pru," I began.

"What?"

"Well, y'know you were pretty funny on Sunday. What did yuh do?"

"Nothin'," said Pru.

"Oh hell. Yuh musta."

"Well, if yuh wanna really know," said Pru, and my heart sank with the same sort of frightened thrill you can get on a swing.

"Go on," I insisted.

"It isn't any of yuh business, Neddy."

"Don't sound so grown up," I said angrily. "It is so my business."

"Well, if yuh must know, nothing did happen—but by golly it nearly did."

"Haw, haw," I tried to jeer.

"No, it didn't, Neddy. We went out to that pub on the cliffs and Norman went and got a bottle of wine and we cleaned it up out in the sandhills. Then he tried to get a bit fresh."

"What about young Quin?" I said hoarsely.

"Norman let him take the car for a spin."

"Haw, haw," I said. "And nothing happened, I s'pose out there in those lonely sandhills? Is that what you're trying to tell me, Pru?"

"Well, yuh know wine," said Prudence. She looked so pretty, it made me feel sick. Now I was getting that sitting in the hay feeling. With sickening clarity, I saw the scene

132

in those desolate sandhills. Wine! You-know! Pru! With those eyelashes! Sometimes I think passion can be compared to a magnifying glass with a lens in direct ratio to blood heat, or specific gravity, or whatever it is that nature has evolved to ensure the propagation of the species. Under her dress, her slim thighs became an acre of pulsating mystery.

"Yes," I said flatly. I knew that she intended to say something further, and if I could have dragged her tongue to a standstill with a handbrake I would have done so. I did not think I would be able to endure what I thought she was going to say.

"Well, if yuh *must* know," she burst out, "I let him. But nothing happened. Don't ask me why. All I know is I'm damn' glad it didn't. It's no credit to me. I'm mighty ashamed of muhself, and speshly what I said to Len Ramsbottom. He's worth six of Norman, flash car and all."

She began to weep.

"Look Prudence," I said, and took her by the arm. "Look dear, you go and tell ole Constable Ramsbottom all about this Salter the Sensational business and tell him yuh awful sorry about Sunday. Don't cry, Pru. Yuh go and see old Len Ramsbottom and betcha everything'll be apples."

"Yuh reckon it might be?" Prudence sobbed.

"Course it will," I said. "You just wait and see. Ole Len's a pretty good guy for a cop. You just see. Everything'll be apples."

I felt pretty mean to Les Wilson, sicking her on to another guy in this way, but whadda hell? Les never had a show anyway. The way I had it figured, if he had failed to make the grade sporting that pith helmet, he never would.

As Prudence whispered goodnight at the door, her eyes bestowed on me a glance of melting gratitude. I squinted back. In the dark once more, it occurred to me that being in the inside bed like this for a change must be a bit like

133

having a holiday. It was hard to believe that the wriggling witch-doctor on the seldom-drawn blind was only the shadow of our old karaka-tree.

That the advice I had given Prudence was sound, was borne out on Monday night by the sporadic clatter of a typewriter in our kitchen. Lessons had resumed.

"What did Len say about Salter the Sensational?" I asked Prudence the next day. Now he was Len! Well, we had a railroad man in the family, why not a cop? The more I reflected on it, the more I liked it. I anticipated a sense of power and reflected glory that would certainly never be generated by my sister drinking wine in the sand-hills with an insurance agent who sported a seven-a-side moustache, even if he did own a white racing car.

"He's gunna find out zactly who he is and keep an eye on him," Prudence informed me. "I'm not to worry about it. In the meantime I'm to come home through town and up Winchester Street. He's nice, eh, Neddy? Isn't he a well-built joker?"

"So's a nelephant," I said, mentally giving up tobacco. "What did he say about Sunday? What'd he say about that awful word you yelled out right in the middle uv the road?"

"Oh, shut up," said Prudence. "Shut up, shut up. I'll never drink wine again, so help me." She had turned the colour of wine. "He was wonderful, Neddy."

"He let you off, huh?"

"Yeah," she lowered her wonderful eyelashes.

"So," I accused. "He got fresh too, huh?"

"He did *not* get fresh," said Pru, but the wine-colour deepened.

"Looks like we gunna have a cop in the family," I sneered. Prudence tossed her head and stalked away. First thing in the morning she looked ever so slightly round-shouldered:

"As well as a railroad man," I shouted after her, and

set off to school with the more objectionable side of my nature positively purring.

That evening just on nightfall, Leonard Ramsbottom, actuated more, I should guess, by the inner radiance of re-union and infatuation than a sense of duty, took it into his head to escort Prudence home, personally. After sitting outside the Quin home in his Austin seven for half an hour or so he decided to inquire within. It was all most unfortunate.

Mrs Quin had driven Tony out to visit a country rela-tive; and, when she had telephoned to say they were stay-ing for tea, her husband, the aged Wooster type whom Angela and I had encountered on our call, had seized the opportunity of pumping a few smooth and rare old liqueurs out of decanters on the sideboard, into my sister. I have no doubt that Prudence tells no more than the truth when she avers she only agreed to sip the drinks be-cause, after all, he *was* Mr Quin and in her eyes the Quins were all that was above reproach, personified. According to Prudence, if Leonard Ramsbottom had been a moment later he would have seen Mr Quin recoiling across the room with his face well slapped, but as a malign fate would have it, this was not the spectacle that greeted the eyes of that stalwart of the Force, as he arrived at the open French windows of the twilit dining-room. So, dazed with surprise at the turn things had taken, and also, no doubt, a little bemused with the deceptive authority of a venerable cog-nac or two, Prudence appeared to be standing, placidly co-operative, balloon glass in hand, while an elderly roué undid her blouse. In a blind burst of rage, which no amount of training in restraint was in time to control, Leonard Ramsbottom leapt across the threshold and gave Mr Quin such an almighty shove that he went flying across the room and there was a great shattering of objects d'art and crystalware, etcetera. He then raised his hand to smack Prudence across the face, but a return to sanity arrested the blow in mid-air. Availing herself of the opportunity, Prudence smacked *his* face.

Desperately she began to button up her blouse. "Look, Len," she gasped.

"Look nothing," snapped the outraged young constable. "You're a harlot!" And with those harsh words, vanished into the gathering dusk. He reappeared an instant later, but it was too gloomy to observe how stricken and woebegone she looked; so, unmollified, he said: "In moi hopinion, this story of men lurking in doorways is a prefabrication and, more likely, just wishful thinking. You're a harlot."

This time he *did* go. And so, a moment later, did Prudence, never more to darken those august portals.

Muttering to herself and making angry chops at space with her small clenched fists, Prudence was half-way along the main street before she realized people were watching her curiously. She fled down an alleyway, wove in and out of narrow lanes and finally sank down on the stump of a macrocarpa-tree. As the turmoil in her mind subsided and her breathing slowed up, the tear drops began to gather, but her self-pity suddenly became transformed into a cold fear. She was alone and, save for a street lamp at the other end of the lane, it was dark.

Behind the main street, on our side, is the oldest part of Klynham. There was a lane which could be walked, as a short cut to our block, but a section of it was very swampy and we seldom used it. Standing amid rusty camellias and crabapple-trees there were a few unoccupied cottages. In one section, choked with fennel and blackberry, all that remained standing was a chimney. The sheds alongside the cottages only just managed to remain upright with assistance from ivy and honeysuckle. There was a blacksmith's forge in the skeleton of a shed, a business which subsisted, as far as Les and I could make out, on the patronage of one important customer, namely the council draught-horse. Through a narrow, foliage-choked gully, flowed the town creek to emerge in a deep, abandoned quarry and then disappear again, enchantingly, into a huge pipe. One of these days Les and I planned, as a supreme adventure, to explore the pipe. A shudder runs down my back as I write. I know now as surely as two and two make four that somewhere in that narrow gully or maybe even in the big pipe itself are *the bones of Sam Finn.*

It was very still. Even from the main street there drifted to Prudence no sounds of traffic. Her skin crawled as she became aware of a sound like slow footfalls. She was too petrified to move. But soon she made out the sound to be water dripping from a tank on one of the derelict buildings huddled in the nearby gloom. With shaky knees she arose. It was only a short dash around a corner and down the alley to the main street, but it involved passing the gloomy, ornate windows of Dabney's funeral parlour and chapel. The grimy windows of the chapel dimly reflected a light on the main street. On this side of the track down to the quarry were the grimly staring doors of the high shed in which, Prudence remembered with horror, the museum-piece hearse was garaged. The opening of the track itself was steeped in menacing darkness. It seemed to Prudence that she was being watched from behind one of the chapel windows, and that, as she stared back, a head was stealthily withdrawn. With a yell of terror she fled back the way she had come and no one before or since ever emerged onto and surveyed the few lights of Klynham's main street with a greater feeling of salvation.

Chapter Thirteen

IT WAS the end of the week before we found out at home that Prudence had quit her job. I do not know what sort of story the amorous Quin told his good lady, but I can imagine he was on shaky ground for a day or two.

On the Thursday Ma said, "I passed Mrs Quin in the main street this afternoon and she cut me dead. Just sailed past me like a gallon on the main street."

"Galleon," I said.

"Galleying she certainly was," declared Ma. "With her nose stuck up in the air like an empty cannon in the park. I can hardly bring myself to credit she did not see me, or overhear me speaking to her very politely, and it is plain to me, as a consequence of being humilified like this on the main street, that she considers herself a cut above the likes of us. And who would she have been, I ask yuh, before she trapped into matrimony this Quin with all his money, but plain Lizzie Haywood, whose father as near as dammit went to jail for stealing a horse? Next time I come across that stuck-up piece of goods I'll let her know in no uncertain manner that, much as she might like to forget her humble early oranges, other memories around Klynham are not so short, even if they are wedded to toilers and junk collectors."

"Please, Natalie," said Pop. "You must refrain from coming to light with such, hrrump, demeaning statements.

The firm of Dee-aitch Poindexter is held in, hrrump, no little esteem in the community. The business world is like a machine and the part played by every cog is of vital importance. The valuing of antiques, their purchase and marketing—"

"Did you say cog," cackled Ma, "or clot? No, Danyel, you're an honest, working man, whose only shortcoming is a predeelectshun for the bottle, though I have always felt my hands are tied in this matter, my own brother, Athol, having led you by the hand through the years into increasingly evil and drunken habits. I've watched it, Danyel, from our early days, even from our wedding day, the shame and mortification of what has left a scar on me forever and a dark cloud in the sky. If I'd had a grain of sense I would have walked away in that beautiful frock and left yuh to marry my brother instead of me, though who would have held yuh up for the ceremony or stooped to soil their hands on the pair of yuh, is beyond me."

"Natalie," said Pop, "I refuse to sit here and listen to yuh bringing up the mistakes of bygone years which, in all conscience, I have tried to repay a thousand times. Hrrump. Natalie—"

The tone of his voice became so different and he cocked his head on one side so sharply that Ma, who was about to sail into him again, said "Yes?"

"Yuh looked beautiful, Natalie," said Pop, "the most beautiful bride that ever was a man's good fortune to behold, let alone have the honour to join in holy mat-re-mahoney. And I, stupid young idiot, blind, stupid young fool, disgraced yuh to a certain extent, being in those days unable to handle my liquor in conjunction with also being intoxicated with yuh beauty."

"Well, well, Danyel," said Ma, looking at my father across the table.

"Are there any more snarlers in the pan?" I said.

"Yuh were the flower of the district, Natalie," said Pop.

"And how yuh ever turned yuh pretty head to look at Dan Poindexter is beyond me and that's a solid fact."

"It's beyond me, *too*," said Ma laughing, but she did not mean what she said. She reached across the table and took Pop's hand. "No, Danyel, yuh may not have been Young Lochnigarry, or whoever I'm thinking of, but yuh were the boy that stole my heart, even if everybody said yuh hadn't two shillings to rub together. A fat lot I cared about money, except to do the right thing for the children, but only for us to be all happy and feel that someone cares whether you're alive or dead."

"My dear," said Pop, "my dearest."

They squeezed hands and then Ma withdrew hers gently, took my plate, got up and went over and dumped another sausage on it.

"Well, Danyel," she said, "we've had our ups and downs and doubtless we're still having 'em, but if we've got love, I'm open to a bet that's more than Lizzie Quin can say with all that dough that dim-wit she married can write his name to. And, when I see her putting on airs in the main street, as if no one remembers that her father was a horse thief, I'll just say to her, 'So yuh riding the high horse a bit today are yuh? Well, I s'pose it runs in the blood and sometimes it comes all over yuh to feel a horse between yuh legs, but make sure it's not night time and in someone else's paddock, Liz *Haywood* Quin!'"

On Friday school broke up for the May holidays at two o'clock in the afternoon and Les and I made our way to the town to celebrate over a milk-shake. We were self-confessed ghouls and we pressed our noses against the window of Charlie Dabney's shop for a moment as we passed, under the pretext of glimpsing Uncle Athol.

Charlie Dabney's business premises ran the whole length of the adjoining alley, the cabinet-making workshop extending three-quarters of the way along, with the chapel and the shed, where the hearse was parked, at the back by the track down to the quarry. On the main street, behind large plate-glass windows, was a display of grimy-looking furniture, which I doubted if any shopper had ever even dreamed of buying, and some wreaths in round glass cases which occasionally, I presumed, were sold whether the customer approved of them or not. Across the alley is the Federal Hotel. Les and I had progressed a few steps past the open doorway when I stopped and went back.

"C'mon," said Les.

"Prudence," I said, looking up the passage. I had glimpsed a very pretty girl leaning against the wall with her hands behind her back and a lock of dark hair over one eye, but it was so unexpected it had called for a double take. She had seen me too and had retreated further up the narrow, uncarpeted passage.

"Prudence," I called again.

She looked around and said desperately, "See yuh after, Eddy."

"Whatchuh doing in there?" I insisted.

"Go'way," she said. I went up the boot-bruised, wooden steps of the Federal Hotel and a little way along the passage, stepping over the heaps of dust and empty cigarette packets. A door was open into the bar and the air was heavy with the smell of spirituous and fermented liquors. If I had found Prudence in an opium den I could not have felt worse about it all. She looked washed-out and big-eyed.

" 'Lo, Neddy," she said in a dispirited way. "Scram willyuh, I'm here on business."

"No, yuh not," I said. "Come along with me."

"Oh yuh don't understand," she said, angrily. "I'll see yuh after."

"You come with me."

"I won't."

We glared at each other and Prudence lowered her eyes. "I won't."

141

"Yes yuh will."

A shadow fell along the passage and there was Les Wilson peering curiously in at us.

" 'Lo, Prudence," he said. I knew he was wishing he had stopped off at home to don his pith helmet.

"C'mon, Pru," I said, urgently, and Pru made a sort of disgusted sound, but she came.

When we got out on the footpath Les said, "Ned and I're gunna have a milk-shake, Prudence. It's my shout, I sold my Hornby train to a guy who thinks he can fix it. That's what *he* thinks. Yuh like a milk-shake, Prudence?"

"Yes, I would," said Prudence. "A strawberry one and I'd like about five hundred ham sandwiches and about a thousand cheese and onion sandwiches and about a million sausage rolls and a—and a pork pie with an egg on it."

We looked at her.

"It was only a little Hornby train," said Les, "and it was broke."

"C'mon, c'mon," said Prudence, and took our arms. "I'll settle for the milk-shake. Maybe I kin eat the straw or something.

"I s'pose yuh all wondering what I was doing in the dump," she said, when we had ensconced ourselves around an iron table with a glass top. "Well now I have to tell yuh that I'm finished up at the Quins' and I don't want Ma to find out until I can say I've got another job. If I can get a job at the pub I can go home and give her some wages and everything will be jake again."

"But Pru," I said. "Hell! Ma wouldn't want you hanging around pubs. When did you finish at the Quins'?"

"Tuesday, I smashed a lot of very val-yoobel things and they growled at me and I walked out and don't tell me I shouldn't've 'cause it's done now and there isn't nothing anyone can do. I don't want Ma all upset and Pop going up to Quin's blowing off steam or something. I just want to get a job and tell Ma I changed because the pay was better. It had better be too, the stingy lot of—"

She put her head down and started to cry a river.

"Buggers," she sobbed. "Stingy lot uv buggers."

Les looked horrified and enchanted at the same time.

"Do yuh mean to tell me," I said, "yuh just been pretending to go to work this week? Yuh mean to tell me yuh been going all day without *eating* anything?"

The waitress brought the milk-shakes Les had ordered and Prudence bit her lip to help control her sobbing, but her face was streaming and the waitress was obviously intrigued. She put down the three milk-shakes and then she came back with a plate so laden she could hardly carry it.

"What the dickens is that?" I said.

"Twenty-eight ham sandwiches," said Les miserably. "It's all uh could afford. That Hornby train was broken, y'know."

I felt sure that I was right when I said that Ma would not relish the idea of her daughter working in an hotel, but Prudence sent Les and me on ahead of her and when she arrived home herself she presented Ma with a fait accompli. In a week's time she was to start at the Federal as a chambermaid. The wages were twice what the Quins paid her. I've forgotten what they were exactly, £2/15/- or something, but I know it seemed princely. Ma was a bit flabbergasted but Prudence's enthusiasm, the increased wage and the poor opinion which Ma now had of Prudence's late mistress, Mrs Quin, all combined to make her capitulate.

"Many's the time," said Ma, "I've said, and I'll say again, that a pub is no place for any daughter of mine to work and if Grandma ever finds out she'll have a fit, but I will say Prudence I admire yuh for yuh interdependence and not standing any nonsense from that horse-stealing Quin creature with her airs and graces, and all the time paying yuh about half what a girl of yuh intelligence could be earning elsewhere. I'll be the last to deny that the money will make a big difference and if my brave girl can use it to buy some nice things for herself why, who knows, what with your typewriting lessons and all, it may not be long before you're in some office or other, Prudence, and we'll be able to look down our snoot at the like of Lizzie Quin, because when all's said and done even if your duties are, as you say, upstairs, the money still comes from the bar downstairs and the likker they sell and the trouble and grief that likker has brought into the world is nobody's bizness."

I thought I saw an unhappy frown come and go on Prudence's countenance when Ma mentioned the typewriting lessons and, now I came to think of it, it was strange we had not seen anything of Len Ramsbottom any night since Monday. A few minutes after Prudence left the kitchen I followed her into her room and to my consternation she was in tears again.

It took me a while to wheedle it out of her, but, in the end, she told me the truth about what had happened at Quin's on the Tuesday night.

"And now," she concluded miserably, "he thinks I'm a"—sob, sob—"hard lot. That's what he called me, a hard lot." Sob, sob.

"P'raps—" I said.

"Never," said Prudence fiercely. "Never. I'd die sooner than speak to him again. If he thinks I'm a hard lot, let him."

She got off the bed and put on her overcoat. She looked wildly around the dilapidated room.

"I'm gunna go for a walk," she said. "I'll go off muh nut if I lie down in this room and think about life. If anybody saw me in this room they wouldn't even be seen speaking to me. They wouldn't think any more of me than a nanimal. That's what they'd think I wuz if they saw this room and this wallpaper. So that's where Pru Poindexter sleeps, does she, they'd think. Well then she's nothing but a nanimal."

I heard the front door close quietly and I know she had gone out that way, so Ma would not see she was howling again.

"What a life," I reflected. Schopenhauer and I would have got along just bully.

I reached out and tore savagely at the hideous roll of rain-and-mildew-blotched wallpaper which billowed down from the ceiling. The repercussions of this impulsive move were out of all proportion. With a loud, tearing sound the entire wall of paper began to rip away from the scrim and sag floorwards. Like an avalanche picking up momentum with its own increasing weight, the ancient paper curved floorwards in a deafening roar and not until it had torn free from the scrim right to the skirting board did it subside at my feet like a dusty, mouldy tent from under which the pole had been wrenched. I gazed at the grotesquely peaked and buckled mountain of paper, open-mouthed. I swallowed hard. I listened. Incredibly, no one outside the room seemed to have heard the din. Furtively I pushed up Prudence's bedroom window and propped it open. Frantically I began to bundle armfuls of paper out through the window. When it was all outside between the house and the fence, and the evening breeze was shaping up to it experimentally, I wiped the sweat off my face, closed the bedroom door and sauntered out through the kitchen, swiping a box of matches on the way.

In which direction to drag it off and burn it? I stood outside the open bedroom window debating this problem. I cursed myself for having overlooked shutting the window. It was not quite dark yet and the wall the paper had peeled off looked stripped and virginal and somehow willing. The more I peered into the room the more inviting the bare expanse of wall seemed to become.

Friday night was late-shopping night in Klynham and

along the wind-chilled streets I sped, coatless, until the windows of A. C. Wilson, Family Merchant, made a bright oasis on a corner in the gathering dusk. It was a nice shop with its uneven floor and low, battered counters, and nice-smelling too, of cheese and chocolate and sausages and ham and oh, everything. You could buy a pound of butter or a hunting knife in a sheath, a frying pan, packet of cinnamon, a hurricane lantern. I had not been too persona grata here for some time; ever since, in fact, Les and I had been ordered to empty our pockets out as we left the shop one afternoon; but my family dealt here and Les was his son, so the genial gleam of Mr Wilson's glasses dimmed only slightly as he nodded to me that Les was in the store-room. A white-aproned Chester Montgomery positively fawned on me as he conducted me through to a corner of the store-room where Les was pumping kerosene from a drum into bottles. Chester Montgomery fawned on everybody; but, as Prudence's brother, I got the full treatment.

Les looked a bit blank, but when I told him it was for Pru he went away and asked his father. Mr Wilson came back with Len.

"I haven't stocked it for a long time, Ned," he said. "But there's six or seven rolls of a remnant here somewhere. Very pretty paper, too, and if I remember right, it's been selvedged and everything. Look in that carton under the shelf there, Les."

This "remnant-selvedge" jazz was so much gibberish to me, but when Les found the wallpaper and held it up for me to see I knew that was it all right.

"It's pretty," I said. "Gee, but that's the prettiest wallpaper I've ever seen. Cop those roses and things. Gee! I'll bet it's dear though, Mr Wilson."

"Oh, it's terribly expensive, Ned," said Mr Wilson. "You could go up town to Hardley and Manning and buy up their whole stock for the price of that wallpaper. You

146

just can't get wallpaper like that, any more. The factories just don't make it any more, Ned. I'll bet you there isn't a store in the whole country has got a single roll of a wallpaper that quality. When you see a wallpaper of that class it makes you realize that things aren't what they used to be, Ned. Probably never be the same again, not when it comes to making wallpaper."

"I guess yuh right at that," I muttered.

"No, sir," said Mr Wilson. "That wallpaper is a real quality product and that's something yuh just gotta expect to pay for, eh?"

"Well, maybe," I mumbled, "I could pay yuh a little a week for the rest of my life or something, but Mr Wilson that paper is just right for this bedroom of Prudence's and I'm sure it wouldn't matter how many I looked at now I'd never be happy with anything else, not now I've seen this special wallpaper."

"Well," said Mr Wilson, "I guess you're intending to hang this wallpaper yourself. You have any idea what's the first thing you need to hang wallpaper?"

"No," I mumbled.

"Paste," said Mr Wilson. "And to make paste you need flour. Now I take it you've got flour at home. Where did you buy that flour, Ned?"

"Why here, I guess. I guess Ma got it here."

"Well," said Mr Wilson, "in that case I'm gunna meet you half-way. This is a family business, Ned and we certainly appreciate it when someone can turn right round and say, without thinking, that something they've got at home came from this store. Like that flour. So do you know what I'm gunna do?"

"No, sir."

"Neddy," said Mr Wilson, and put his hands under his apron to stop his belly from shaking loose with laughing, "I'm gunna *give* you that paper. Yes sir, *give* it to you and I want you to tell everybody in town that that's the sorta

147

gesture of appreciation you can expect from A. C. Wilson, Family Merchant."

When Les told me he intended to help as soon as he had filled a few more bottles with kerosene, I nearly burst my boiler getting home to rip the remaining wallpaper down, and generally make Prudence's bedroom presentable for a working-bee. Ma must have thought I had gone stark, staring, but she dropped everything she was doing the moment she cottoned on. She pitched-in making paste, still talking about how the new wallpaper reminded her of the parlour in Grandma Cudby's old house that was burnt to the ground. I have to hand it to Ma. Without her I would not have stood a chance of papering that room, but Ma was a dynamo, doing everything at once and talking nineteen to the dozen. To my everlasting astonishment, Pop pitched in too when he arrived, but he had a few under his belt and got in our road as much as anything. We were short of a stepladder and this is where Les Wilson showed his mettle. The stud was pretty high in that old house, but Les was like a monkey standing tip-toe on the top of the bed-end, while I stood on a chair on top of a washstand. We worked like demons, but I never thought for a moment we could ever finish the job before Prudence arrived home. We expected her about 9.30 when the shops shut, but when this time went by and there was still no sign of her, we figured she must have gone to see a film, which gave us another hour. By eleven the room was done, but there was still no Prudence and my frantic delight was becoming tinged with worry.

Les and I hung her little picture up on the wall again and Ma came in with some geraniums in a glass jar and put them by the bed. She took the tattered rug off the floor and replaced it with one in better condition that must have been in her and Pop's room. I was a bit disappointed at the paper not looking tighter and I did not like the dark, wet patches spoiling the pattern, but both Ma and

Pop said it would be O.K. when it dried out. I hoped they were right. Any way you would never have believed it was the same room. With the window open and the curtains blowing in and out, and the rose-covered walls, it could have been a room at the Quins' or Josephine McClinton's. It looked too good to be true. But where was Prudence?

We had a cup of tea and some toast. It was half-past eleven by this time, but Les said no, he'd be damned if he would go home before Prudence saw the room. I know how he felt. I wandered up and had another look at the room, and, to my joy, Ma and Pop were right when they said it would dry out and tauten. It looked wonderful. If only Prudence would come home. There was something sad about the way the curtains blew in and out of the neat, bright, empty room.

Then I heard Ma calling me in an urgent stage whisper and I just got out to the kitchen as I heard footsteps on the veranda. She went to the washhouse first.

"You get under the table, Les," I said. "Quick. She'll smell a rat if she sees you here at this time of night."

As it was, Prudence looked most surprised to see Ma and Pop and me sitting around the table. She looked very dejected.

"Whatcha all doing up?" she said.

"Having a cuppa," said Ma promptly. "Like a cuppa, Prudence?"

"Awright," said Prudence wearily. Ma poured her out a cup and Prudence, who was standing by the table with her legs about a foot from Les's face, then said, "I'll take it into my room, Ma, and drink it in there. I'm pretty tired. Ni', ni', Ma, Pop, ni', ni', Neddy."

She kissed Ma, and took the cup and away she went. Les came out from under the table grinning like a halfwit. We heard the light go click in her room and then there was a long silence. Then she burst into the kitchen and her

149

eyes were like saucers. Doggone it, I hate admitting this, but I may even have been on the verge of blubbing myself, I was so happy.

Prudence just looked at us all stupidly.

"Well," said Ma. "Do you like it Pru?"

"I dunno what to say," said Prudence. It was a fact that she looked absolutely flabbergasted.

"However didya do it so quick?" she said. "Where didya get that pretty wallpaper? I thought I was in the wrong house. Ma, Eddy, Pop, I dunno what to say. It's *wonderful*."

She kissed us all and, as a matter of pure routine the way things were lately, started blubbing again. That was only to be expected. Les got an extra big kiss and after that it looked to me as if he had no intention of going home at all that night. It looked to me as if he was getting ready to settle right in and paper the whole house.

Chapter Fourteen

HOLIDAYS have been defined as a time spent wondering if one would not be better off somewhere else and doing something different; but this May, fate seemed to have everything cut and dried. It was a case of the more you stir the more you stink. Prudence's bedroom now laughed at the rest of the house and the kitchen now looked unbearably dingy in our eyes.

"What say we paint it?" said Prudence, eyeing the kitchen on Saturday morning. "There's tins and tins half-full of paint in the old shed."

She was right. There were dozens of tins and most of them gallon tins at that, down in the old shed. Pop had apparently stumbled across all this paint at some time or other on his travels and piled it all on the truck, just in case. There were even some brushes soaking in a tin of stagnant water. It was difficult to read the label on some of the tins and the contents all looked the same, like brown oil, but we stirred and stirred and gradually the brown oil churned into rich, creamy paint. There were some tins of red roof paint, which appeared to have never been opened. I dismissed a fleeting doubt concerning Pop's sense of distinction between tweelemeum and tweedle-teum (or something. I am unable to find it in any of my reference books) as unworthy of me.

" 'Y'know something," I said. "There's enough paint here to do the whole flippin' house."

"Well," said Prudence, "why don't we paint the whole flippin' house?"

We stared at each other and then down at the tins of paint. Thoughtfully, Prudence began to pull up her dress and tuck it into her knickers. "Well," I thought, "this'll teach me to keep my big mouth shut. Here goes the May vacation."

When I walked out of the shed, carrying two tins of paint, my heart sank. The house looked as big as the government buildings. I thought, better nip this in the bud and call it off right away before we start wasting our time. I put down the paint and turned around to face Prudence, who was following me with the tin of water that had the handles of the brushes sticking up out of it. One look at my sister and I picked up the paint again and kept walking. She looked ruthless.

By four o'clock in the afternoon I was thoroughly enjoying myself. By mutual agreement Les and I postponed our visit to the cinema and the current episode of "The Fire God's Treasure" until the evening session.

Oh yes, by this time Les was on the job with us. And so also, I might point out, were Chester Montgomery, butcher boy Herman, and Pop. This was the team that coped with the really big areas; but also, playing their part, were Ma and Angela Potroz, who painted the veranda and the more easily reached places. I can still see sweet-natured Angela down on her knees all on her own, around the shadowed front of the house, earnestly scraping the moss off the ventilation boards, with her paint can in readiness beside her.

We painted right through Sunday, the full gang, even Herbert, although Ma went inside and hid as the cars began to arrive outside the Temple of the Brethren of the Lamb. She concealed herself again later on when the service broke up and the worshippers started up their vehicles to go home.

Uncle Athol painted a few boards in the afternoon and then he went away to borrow a blowlamp; and ta-ta, Uncle Athol.

The weather was perfect for painting, fine but cool, after heavy frosts in the early morning. By Monday, Les and I were painting the roof, and it was marvellous up there. The air seemed fresh and the town, seen from above, looked different somehow, wide-spread and dreaming. We could see the old Fitzherbert mansion, and, among the pines, our old shed where we had not ventured (well not to speak of anyway, oo-hoo that applejack) since the brush with the Lynchites. Josephine McClinton went past and in a weak moment, while having a smoke behind the chimney, I confessed to Les I was nuts about her. Well, I guess that made us square, but at least he had a friend at court. My case looked pretty hopeless. Josephine's ivory tower was high, like a skyscraper is high, and I had a feeling I would need a brass band rather than a guitar to go serenading her.

The five-fifty twenty-one situation had reached an all-time zero and, with the Dennis smugly immobilized in the yard, Pop and Herbert spent the day helping Prudence give the walls a second coat. By evening, one could hardly credit it was the same house. The second coat made all the difference. The old, dry wood just guzzled up the first coat. Angela Potroz had taken it upon herself to do all the window facings and sills and a very artistic job she was making of it. Just after five o'clock, as soon as they finished work, Chester and Herman turned up to do what they could before nightfall. Chester even came for a little while in the dinner hour, but the call of the nose-bag was strong and he accomplished very little.

Tuesday there were just Les and me, Prudence and Angela, working. It was extremely peaceful and a happier little team–would not have been found anywhere.

We decided to make an early start on the Wednesday in an effort to cut the job out. We decided that after Angela had gone home after tea. Les had stayed for tea too. Ma was so pleased with us and so proud of the house she seemed dazed. She put up a terrific spread for tea. The gastrological cards Ma could deal off the bottom of the pack in emergencies never failed to amaze me. I had known mincemeat was due, but the dumplings took the wind out of my sails.

There was another snorter of a frost in the morning so Les and I were unable to mount the roof first thing. The three of us were just deciding which of the remaining unpainted areas to tackle when Uncle Athol and Charlie Dabney arrived on the scene. Time, 7.45. Charlie Dabney had a bottle of brandy sticking out of his pocket and Uncle Athol clutched the blow-torch he had set out to borrow on Sunday afternoon. Ma appeared on the veranda, hands on hips.

"And what have you got there, Athol, at this hour of the day?"

"Ah, hah, Natalie," burbled Uncle Athol, "a blow-torch m'dear. Soon have the job done now. Thought ole Athol had forgotten, but never on yuh life. Not Athol."

"Not Athol," burbled Charlie Dabney. "Not ole team AtholnCharlie, Miz Dee-aitch, not AtholnCharlie."

He tottered around and began opening and shutting his hands. Uncle Athol put the blow-torch under his arm and began opening and shutting his hands as well. The blow-torch fell to the ground.

"Cremation arrainsh," they chanted. "Cremaish arrainsh, cremaish arrainsh."

"Oh what's the use," stormed Prudence and bolted inside the house, past Ma.

"Soon have the job done," roared Ma. "I like that, yuh drunken clot. Too inebriated at this hour of the morning

154

to look around and see that the job *is* done, thanks to Prudence and Eddy. What an hour to come staggering up the path with a blowfly torch, or whatever it is, and start talking about finishing the job. I can well imagine what finishing the job would mean in your inebriated eyes, Athol Cudby, and that's probably burn the house down to the ground around our ears like Grandma's house (if Grandma could see you now at this hour of the morning!) just when we're all so proud of looking a bit respectable for once in our lives. 'Finish the job!' "

With a snort of infinite disgust Ma retired, doubtless to console the temperamental Prudence.

"Episode closed, episode closed," said Charlie to Uncle Athol. "Have a brandy ole soulmate, have snort brandy to 'leviate gloom, dispel sorrow, and so on and so on. Episode closed."

"Well I'll be damned if I'll paint the house, now," said Uncle Athol. "Damned if I'll lift a finger to help them paint the house if they crawled to me on their knees, begging for me to use this here blow-torch."

"Thas spirit," said Charlie. "Man's got his pride after all. But never do the balls, Athol ole boy. Have brandy, reconsider, reflect, forgive transgresh against as forgive et cetera. AND so on and so on, so on. Episode closed. Prosheed according to plan."

Much pleased with his oration, Charlie Dabney subsided into an imperceptible chair, and somersaulted in the direction of the gully-trap. He fell heavily. He could have killed himself for all I cared. Disgusted and ashamed, I beckoned Les to follow me, and we went around the back of the house.

The frost was still on the ground and it was going to take an effort to remove our hands out of our pockets and start to paint. The Uncle Athol-Charlie Dabney act had undermined our morale somewhat, taken in conjunction with Prudence going inside to sulk, and our hands stayed in our pockets. We crouched down on our haunches in a patch of sunlight and had a moody conversation. Ma rapped on the window. I said to Les, "C'mon and let's have a cuppa anyway. Then maybe we'll get cracking."

I was relieved to see Prudence sitting up at the end of the kitchen table, her good temper apparently restored. In fact she was actually laughing at Charlie Dabney who was sitting up at the table half-asleep but still master of ceremonies over an almost incredibly idiotic conversation-piece.

Pop and Herbert were standing by the coal range eating toast with their cups of tea on the mantelpiece. Pop was doing his best to be polite to old Charlie, but it was taking him all his time.

"Great Scott, Dee-aitch," said Charlie. "Incredible. Fansh being together to break our fast over the festive board and that buyhoofal flower of the wilderness"— indicating a giggling Prudence—"being among those present. It's an ill wind that blows no one over, Dee-aitch, a long lane that hasn't got a worm in it." He peered owlishly around. "Wheresh Athol?"

I looked around also and Ma said to me in an aside, "Yeruncle is doing the front door with his blowfly torch. I tried to stop him, but anything for a quiet life on the ocean wave as the saying goes."

As soon as I opened the kitchen door I heard the roaring of the blow-torch. Uncle Athol was sitting on the doorstep with the door open into the passage and he was subjecting the panels of the door to a fierce, blue jet of flame. He had the blow-torch in one hand. With the other he was following the glowing trail of the flame with the blade of a kitchen knife. No doubt about it, he was ripping off the old paint beautifully. Even Angela had mentioned the lamentable condition of the front door and had so far baulked at tackling it. Wonders would never cease. The old Uncle had some use after all.

156

I had only just got back into the kitchen when Prudence stood up and said, "C'mon, c'mon, let's get on the job." Les followed her out like a dog, but I gulped down my tea first. Nobody was going to hustle me along. Still gasping, I joined Prudence and Les in the yard.

"Up yuh go on the roof," said Prudence imperiously. "And then I'll need the ladder to finish off that bit up there."

That left Les and me marooned on the roof.

"You do that bit," said Les. "I'll finish off over there."

It was beginning to look like I was just the rouseabout round this place. Grimly I set to work, keeping at least one foot jammed against every lead-headed nail I could see. It was about half an hour later that I noticed the wisps of smoke coming up over the edge of the roof and drifting playfully around my brush. A few minutes later I woke up.

"Hey," I yelled. "Prudence! Bring the ladder! Hey! Help! The house is on fire. Bring the ladder, Pru, get the fire-brigade, ring the phone! Hey, Les! We're trapped on the roof and the derned house is going up in smoke."

Keep cool, I thought.

"Prudence!" I screamed. "Over here, round here with the ladder, get the fire-brigade, yuh goof, and get me outa here, we're going up in smoke!"

Relax, I thought; keep calm, the captain is the last to leave the ship. Prudence appeared below me, brush in hand.

"You idiot," I remarked placidly. "Bring the ladder willyuh before I'm roasted alive on the roof and ring the fire-brigade and *bring the ladder*. Can't you see THE WHOLE FRIGGIN' HOUSE is on fire!"

Les did something I would never have dared to have done. He jumped. Prudence staggered round with the ladder to where I had been painting and I retreated in good order, apart from forgetting my brush and paint can.

157

From the ground there was no smoke to be seen and I began to think I had made an ass of myself properly, but Prudence was white-faced and panting.

"The place is on fire!" she hooted. "Uncle Athol has set the house on fire! Do something, willyuh. Ma's stuck in the hedge trying to use the phone next door, but there's no one home. Do something, willyuh!"

And so it came to pass that yours truly E. C. Poindexter (Neddy) had the pleasure of smashing the glass on the emergency fire alarm fixed to the telegraph pole right outside the front door of the Temple of the Brethren of the Lamb. I pressed the button and waited for the town to blow up. From here our beautifully painted house on the corner was wreathed in clouds of curling smoke. I sank helplessly down in the gutter. The ghost of my spiritual sparring partner, Schopenhauer, sat down alongside me.

"Here we go again," he remarked. "See what I mean, Bud?"

There were only two Dennis products in Klynham. One of them was our little old tip-truck and the other was the big fire-engine. They were both ancient models, in fact it would not surprise me to learn that the fire-engine was the earlier of the two, but what a thrill I got when the old red monster came screaming around the bend and began to thunder up Winchester Street, all its brass glittering in the morning sunlight and the banshee really going to town. They were probably not going very fast, really, but what a psychological effect that howling banshee has! I reckon Malcolm Campbell would have pulled the Bluebird over to let them past even if he had to sit there and roll a cigarette while he waited.

The whole town, including Josephine McClinton, arrived a minute or two after the Dennis. I went and sat in the shed, I was so ashamed. I never loved Prudence so much as I did when her shadow in the shaft of the sunlight through the half-open door was followed by herself and she sat down gloomily and inelegantly on a box beside me. It was a long time before the shouting died away and then, by tacit agreement, we emerged.

Not much damage had been done. The front door no longer needed blow-torching, being now non-existent; the paint in front of the house needed a touch up, the passage was full of foam and water and wallpaper and the ceiling was black and charred, but otherwise everything was hearteningly intact. The Poindexters still had a roof over their heads and a newly painted one to boot.

"Many's the time," declared Ma, presiding over the most amazing collection of guests our kitchen had ever harboured, "I've said that fire was worse than earthquake, or war, an idea I've laboured in my bosom since Grandma's house was raised from the ground by fire and the impression it left on my mind forever."

"What a party," said Charlie Dabney. "Great Scott, the lights won't go out all night."

Fortunately he fell asleep again.

"Help yourselves," said Ma. "It isn't often that I approve of people reparticipating in the demon rum at this hour of the day, but if ever there was an emergency this is it by Jesus, if you'll forgive me, Reverend?"

The Reverend Higgins wagged his head.

"Just a small one," he said to Prudence, who was sloshing the Dabney brandy around in great style. "As your mother says, an emergency like this calls for some resilience in our attitude to what is right and proper in the Lord's eyes. My dear, do have a glass yourself, after your fearful ordeal in the flame in which apparently"—the Reverend coughed discreetly—"you have lost your garments. Bless us all, and restore us to our rightful heritage of warm garments to clothe our limbs, and to comfort and safety from the devouring tongues of fire, so recently defeated by our gallant, not to say noble, firemen."

159

"Cheers," said a big man, whose brass helmet was on the table.

"Cheers," said the Reverend Higgins still looking at Prudence who, I may have forgotten to mention, was wearing the same dress she had worn out in the racing car with the insurance bloke. She looked like Tarzan's soulmate. She jammed me up against the mantelpiece by sticking the muzzle of the brandy bottle in my stomach.

"Have one yourself, sport," she said hoarsely. "After yuh ordeal in the flames and what-have-yuh, you've earned one. I may even indulge, hrrump, myself."

She tilted up the bottle and drank till her eyes glazed over. So did I. She heaved, then grabbed the bottle off me and partook of another mighty draught. So did I. Then we excused ourselves. Only the fresh air saved us from vomiting it all up. On the patch of garden around the end of the house we hung around each other's necks and laughed until the tears streamed down our faces. This is how we were when Len Ramsbottom found us.

Len was visibly moved by our pale, tear-ravaged countenances and the babes-in-the-wood hold we had on each other.

"Hallow me," he said, "to offer moi most sincere sympathy for the trouble you have had this mah-horning. Through-out the week Oi 'ave noticed the most commend-ah-hable way you 'ave both worked at pah-hainting the 'ouse. Hallow me to conher-gratulate you. These things are sent to try us out, Miss Poindexter, er, Prudence, and I am grateful that no great-her damage has he-ventuated. I 'ave taken a brief statement from your mother pertaining to the houtbreak of fire and I 'ope to be seeing you in the hemmediate future with an eye"—he blushed—"to rehahsuming our toipewriting le-hessons."

He looked an awfully big man, with a sort of clumsy dignity that was all his own, as he went around the end of the house.

160

Chapter Fifteen

To give an idea how resilient we were, to borrow from the vocabulary of the Rev. Higgins, we were painting again before dinner hour. Prudence was a new girl on the strength of Len Ramsbottom's affable address. We waved to literally hundreds of sightseers. A fire was a big event in these parts, and, ordinarily, our fire would have been a subject of jesting talk for many months. Little we knew that a blackly scowling fate planned otherwise.

Pop went and lay down for the afternoon. He and Herbert had been at the other end of the town changing a wheel on the Dennis when they heard the house was on fire, and their panic-stricken activities from then on had left Pop in a nerve-shattered and debilitated condition. Herbert was more resilient and went and played snooker. Uncle Athol was in bed, taking refuge from disgrace in swinish slumber.

Mr Wilson had clamped down on Les in the afternoon to do some deliveries around the town. We were discussing the relative merits of sandsoap, linseed oil and turpentine for removing paint off our hands and arms, when Herbert came up the steps between us and went inside, without answering our greeting. He was not looking as resilient as he might have been.

"What's biting him?" said Prudence. I shrugged and went on picking paint off a knuckle, and then Prudence

161

nudged me, and said, "He wants yuh." I followed Herbert into our room. He sat down on the edge of the bed and I could see he was mightily perturbed over something.

"Look, Neddy," he said, "I'm in the cart good and proper. If I learned one lesson today it's this, and yuh better listen 'cause one day yuh might thank me for telling yuh, and that's this—never play snooker for money with a guy that carries his own chalk in his pocket."

"Yuh owe some money?" I said, astutely.

"Yuh telling me I owe some money," said Herbert, hoarsely. "Eight quid. Where am I gunna get that sorta dough from? I've borrowed three quid from Jack Glen, but a fiver, who in hell's gunna lend me a fiver?"

"Don't pay him," I said.

"Yuh don't understand," groaned Herbert. "Everyone in the room watched this last game for a tenner. Kelly, Hodson, everyone. I thought I could whack the arse off this spivvy-looking character. I thought the way he played the first three games for a dollar and then ten bob he was a pushover. I thought he was nuts when he said, 'Let's play for a tenner.' I thought it was money for jam. It's the oldest trick in the world and big sucker me falls for it. I should've known when I saw he carried his own chalk. I tell yuh, Neddy, I'm in the cart and that's fuh sure. He's out to make trouble, this character. If I haven't got that money this evening I'll have to shoot through. I just couldn't face the boys again if I welsh on this lot. There's nothing for it, Neddy, I'll just have to shoot through and it serves me right for being so dern stupid as to play a guy that carries his own chalk. It oughter be about the first lesson a guy oughter be taught, as soon as he gets outa short pants, and that's look out for a guy that carries his own chalk. But it's too late to talk about it now. I'm washed up around this neck uv the woods."

"How about ole Charlie Dabney?"

Herbert gave me a peculiar look.

162

"Well, Neddy," he said, and sighed, "if yuh must know I've approached old Charlie."

"And he knocked you back?" I said.

"Well no, not really," said Herbert. "Oh hell, let's forget it, I'll just pack muh grip and shoot through."

"Go on—what did he say? If he didn't knock yuh back, what did he say?"

"He said—oh hell."

"Go on, spill it."

"Well," said Herbert, "he said—oh hell, he's pissed to beat the band and he said sure I could have a fiver, anything to oblige a son of Dee-aitch and all that bunk, but he'd feel happier if he presented it, personally, to Prudence."

"To Prudence!" I exclaimed.

"Yeah to Prudence! The flower of the wilderness. The beautiful waif of the tempest or something. I tell yuh, Neddy, the ole coot's off his rocker, he's going around the bend."

"Prudence!" I exclaimed again.

"Who's talking 'bout me?" said Prudence, looking in suspiciously.

Herbert looked down at the floor in shame, so I started in and gave her the whole story.

"Well, I'll be blowed," she said. "He wants to give *me* a fiver."

"It's for me, really," said Herbert, hastily.

"Oh yes, I know that. Well, why doesn't he give it to you? Oh well, I suppose I'd better put on another frock and we'll go an' see the silly old tit."

"Will yuh really, Pru?" said Herbert. "Gee, Pru, I'll never forget this. As soon as I get some money it's all yours."

"She's right," said Prudence.

"Look here, Pru," began Herbert.

"What?"

"Well I mean to say I don't want ole Charlie trying to kiss you or something."

"That'll be the day," said Prudence. "He better not. I'll have to kid him a bit, I s'pose, but none of that kissin' business. Help, I reckon his breath ud knock yuh down flat on yuh back."

She went out and Herbert sprang up. He looked a new man.

I went with them. By the time we arrived at Charlie Dabney's place of business, Prudence was not looking so keen.

"Can't this wait till termorrow?" she muttered.

"Not really," said Herbert. "Gee, I know he's in there, Pru, and who's frightened of that little fatty?"

"It's not him I'm scared of," said Pru, looking at the dark windows. "It's that awful place. No wonder he drinks. To live in that place you'd want to be blind-shickered all the time."

"But he is," said Herbert, who was not really listening, he was trying so hard to see a sign of light behind the grimy plate-glass windows. "He definitely is."

He went over and tried the front door. It opened with a creak.

"Oooh," said Prudence.

As we stood there in the deepening twilight the street lights flickered into life along the main street.

"C'mon," said Herbert. "Eddy and I'll stand inside the door." The three of us stood inside the door and Herbert called out, "Mr Dabney, Mr Dabney."

We stood for a moment and then, somewhere at the back of the shop, we heard shuffling footsteps.

"There he is," urged Herbert. "Go on, Pru, don't be a baby, we're here."

Boldly Pru walked across the front shop and around the end of the counter. The only light in the shop was from the street. Prudence vanished. We heard her footsteps stop. Next thing she was back.

"Out! Out!" she yelped and plunged past us into the street. We followed her and, inadvertently, I pulled the door so sharply the Yale lock clicked shut.

"Well, now yuv done it!" said Herbert angrily.

"Done nothing," snapped Prudence. "Wild horses won't drag me back into that chamber uv horrors. She-whit the place is full of coffins and, Eddy, you know who I think I saw?" I felt a shiver explore my spine.

"No," I whispered.

"Salter the Sensational," said Prudence and her eyes were like that character on the glory road, like moons. "Standing among the *coffins*."

"She-whit."

"Now I'm sunk," gloomed Herbert. "As if I didn't have enough trouble without you two kids to start in seeing things. I tell yuh I was around here only an hour ago and if there was one coffin there, that's all. One measly coffin and the girl jumps out of her pants."

"Yuh leave my pants outa this," flashed Prudence. "It's you that wantza kick in the pants for losing that money. If it wasn't for you I wouldn't have to go through a nordeal like this. Five quid. Yuh wouldn't get me back in that chamber uv horrors for five thousand quid and yuh can play that over on yuh ukelele."

"Shut up," hissed Herbert. "Shut up, will yuh, here's the guy I owe the dough to, coming down the street now."

There now hove into view the most jaunty-walking, flashy-dressed, spivvy-looking character I had ever seen. He was about medium height, but he was as skinny as a gadget for getting corks out of bottles. This rooster was no heavier than I was, I would calculate, but the shoulders of his check suit were a mile wide. The brim of his hat was more like an umbrella with the wind under it than the brim of a hat. The hat had a feather sticking up out of the band like an ostrich plume. He was smoking a cigarette in a six-inch holder, and, when he took it out of his mouth to blow out smoke and flick the ash off the end, he flung his arm out in front of him and looked at it as if he were the man who broke the bank at Monte Carlo. He was not so much walking as dancing, rising up on tiptoe with each step, and the advancing leg flicking out from the knee like a whip. The thumb of the hand that was not busy gesticulating with the cigarette holder, was hooked into a waistcoat that looked like one of those coloured charts of the circulatory system I endeavour not to notice, in the medical journal. From my point of view this individual's total ensemble was something I would have liked to turn the page over on quickly, but he paused when he came up to us. He made an elegant bow.

"Salutations," he proclaimed in a twangy voice. "And who, Herbert, is this luscious morsel? Holding out on me, huh? Who would have thought it in a burg like this? What a piece of lush brush! This sheila oughta be a film actress. What a clarse piece of arse! Herbert, you're the luckiest guy in the world to find a supercharged hunk of gashed stuff like this in a burg like Klynham. I can't wait to shake the dust of this Gawd-forsaken burg off my little tootsie wootsies; but first, of course, there is a little matter of eight, teeny, weeny quidlets you owe me and which I would like to take possession of pronto, if not sooner."

He looked at Prudence, pushed his hat back and rocked on his heels. He shot his arm out and flicked ash away.

"What a filly! What a waste to see a broad like you go to seed in this Gawd-forsaken burg. With a bod like that, baby, you'n I could really make the towns and hit the high spots. This junk-head here is numb from the ears up, no offence ole cock-a-doodle, but reely trooly a guy who handles a koo like you, just don't deserve a curvy little piece of homework like this here gorgeous, bouncy, juicy —reely you're the most, sister, you're the most."

Herbert was shaking with rage. Suddenly the stranger left off rocking backwards and forwards and running his eyes up and down Prudence. He wheeled on Herbert.

"Where's this dough, cock-a-doodle?" he said, showing his teeth. "You've had long enough to raise the ante, sport. C'mon, give, give."

He held out his hand. He was only a runt, but I will candidly admit he scared me. He looked the most likely type to pack a gat I had ever seen.

"Uh sure like yuh, big boy," said Prudence.

We all looked at her. She waggled her hips and the hair slipped down over her eye. "Yessuh," she cooed. "Yuh sure look like a real, live man to me, yessuh. Yuh look like a man that might know how to give a girl a good time and not fool about like the yokels around these parts. Cop that classy suit. I sure do like a man that knows how to dress like a man, and not look like something outa Snake Gully."

Prudence ran her eye over poor Herbert and wrinkled her nose. Her lower lip curled.

"What a waste of time," she said, witheringly. "What a dead-loss, smalltown hobo yuh look standing alongside a man that knows the answers and knows what a girl craves for."

Herbert, mouth open, sagged as if he had stopped a kick in the solar plexus.

Prudence now commenced the sort of hip action that goes with hula-hooping.

"Yuh know what a girl craves for, big boy," she said.

"Sister," said the stranger, holding her arm by the elbow and looking into her eyes, "I'll hand it to yuh, yuh know yuh own mind and yuh making no mistake. Yuh met up with a citizen that'll cover yuh with diamond rings and fill yuh up with champagne, a real man that knows what a honeybunch like yuhself craves for and is equipped to satisfy that craving. From now on yuh life is just a bed of

167

roses, honeh chile, just a bed of roses. A sexy little piece like you is wasted on these hoboes. We'll make the big smoke together, sweetheart, and just wait till the boys see the class bit of grummit I've picked up for muhself in the sticks, of all places."

"Yuh wonderful," breathed Prudence.

"Hold it, sister," said the big-shot, patting her arm. He turned to Herbert. He laughed tinnily. "Well, small-time, yuv cut your stick. Now give us this dough and wave us good-bye. Get yuhself a tame goat, Herby, and learn to play croquet or something. Yuh way outa yuh class, Herby. Now *fork up*."

Prudence pulled his arm, "Listen, muscles," she said, "let's not have any trouble here in the street, huh? Ain't I coming along with yuh? Ain't that enough? This poor boob'll prob'ly cut his throat losing me like this, and just between us he hasn't got peanuts. C'mon, muscles, a few quid is only nuthin' to a big-shot from the smoke. Let's just change the scenery, huh, and leave this yahoo with his memories."

"So yuh ain't raised the wind, eh, sport?" said Flash Freddy. His eyes narrowed. "So yuh just a small-time, welshing punk, eh? A man ought to let the daylight through a no-account two-timing chiseller like you."

"Look here," cried Herbert, trying to fit into the act.

"Look here nuthin'," snarled Flash Freddy. "You're a welsher. Yuh must have *some* dough."

Miserably, Herbert groped into his pocket and produced a couple of pound notes. They were snatched out of his hand.

"Yuv taken my sheila, haven't yuh?" said Herbert. "Yuv ruined my life. Isn't that enough?"

"Listen to the punk," sneered Prudence. "C'mon, muscles. Let's walk the dog."

Flash Freddy emitted his tinny cackle. He patted Prudence.

"Yuh sure are some baby. O.K., kid. Let's amble somewhere and get acquainted. This sort of mug makes my belly heave."

He offered Prudence his bent arm and she looked up admiringly at him as she hooked onto him.

"Let's blow, muscles," she breathed. "I can hardly wait."

Away they strutted down the street and Herbert and I gazed after them in awe. Behind her back, Prudence signalled violently to us with her free hand.

"Jumping cats," gulped Herbert, "is she a smooth worker or is she! How's she gunna get rid uv'm?"

"She'll fix him, awright," I grinned. I had a lot of confidence in Prudence. Then my grin became a ghastly grimace. Constable Len Ramsbottom in full regalia had appeared on the corner and, in a thunderstruck sort of way, was observing Prudence and her escort approaching. As they went past, Flash Freddy's arm shot out and a piece of ash floated in the general direction of the constable. We heard a tinny cackle of derisive laughter.

Chapter Sixteen

WITH the painting finished except for a few out-of-the-way corners, which never ever did get painted, and Prudence not due to start work at the Federal Hotel until Monday, the three of us (that is, Prudence, Les and me) had a few days of just mooching about. Most of the time Angela Potroz mooched with us. We walked along the railway track in both directions (on different occasions, that is); we explored gullies and looked for eels in creeks that flowed in the shadow of the willows; we crossed the creeks on fallen logs, we sat on a monument in an overgrown Domain; we climbed trees, we found a little cave. A favourite place of ours became a bracken-covered bank high over the main road south, and from here we looked down on the hoods of passing automobiles and, I may as well admit, spat on them or tried to. We must have become a familiar foursome mooching about the back streets of Klynham. Sometimes we sat in the gutter and chewed straws. We were all broke.

We had four days of this glorious existence, the only interlude being on Saturday afternoon when Prudence and Angela played basketball and Les and I went to the cinema and plunged down the peril-strewn jungle trails in quest of the Fire God's treasure. We called for the girls after the matinee and I think we both kicked ourselves for not having spent the afternoon watching the basketball games. I know I did, and it is significant that Les suggested that, as, in his opinion, one got more for one's money at the evening session, we should attend the cinema at night on Saturdays from now on. Watching basketball was hardly an approved pastime for the boys of the village, but Les and I had a wonderful alibi in sister Prudence and friend Angela.

All the girls wore long black stockings and the most abbreviated gymnasium frocks imaginable. Most of the girls wore stockings that were almost transparent, they were so threadbare, and this inadvertent sheerness of texture enhanced the allure of the ripe, blooming flesh on calf and thigh. Josephine McClinton had a new pair of stockings, which was a pity, but her frock was in open competition with the others for skimpiness. The inch or two of upper leg, which was all the frocks attempted to conceal, got very little privacy in the heat of the game, and moreover the girls seemed to be forever adjusting their garters or suspenders and yanking at their stocking tops. Believe me, it was better than the can-can. Leaning over the fence watching the basketball, Les and I cheered as lustily as anyone, but we knew not who was winning, or what they were trying to do.

Prudence started at the Federal on Monday and we missed her badly, but we kept on mooching. She had not reproached Herbert or me in the slightest way for having been really responsible for her final disastrous encounter with Len Ramsbottom. She seemed to be past caring. She told me that Flash Freddy had bought two tickets for the little train which went through Klynham at ten o'clock at night to link up with the express at Te Rotiha. She had got on the car with him and then, at the last minute, got off again. As simple as that. What a girl!

On Saturday afternoon, the last Saturday in the holidays, Les and I leaned over the wire fence again and watched the basketball games. Prudence finished work for the week at mid-day on Saturdays. The days were still fine after frosts, but it was beginning to get very raw and cold as early as mid-afternoon. Winter was bringing up the big guns. A whole afternoon of watching the basketball players took a lot out of Les and me—more, I would not be surprised, than if we, ourselves, had played Rugby for the same period of time. I know Prudence and Angela seemed full of beans and skylarked the whole way on the walk back to town, but Les and I just ambled along. We were half-way along the main street which was practically deserted, as was usual with the shops closing at mid-day, when a bicycle corps swept silently up beside us, dismounted and propped their machines along the kerb. We were in the hands of the Philistines. Nearly the whole Lynch gang surrounded us.

"Hey, what's the idea?" said Les, very pale.

"You know what the idea is, Wilson," said Victor Lynch menacingly. "Poindexter knows too, so don't try any tricks."

"Got yourself a couple of sheilas, eh?" said big Clem Walker.

"Look at Prudence's legs," I heard Peachy giggling. "Oh boy! They're better than skinny ole Potroz's."

"We're going down to the shed," said Lynch. "All of us. Nobody's gunna get hurt. We're just gunna have a little fun."

"Think you're the only guys in Klynham got any right to sheilas," said Skin Hughson. "Y'got another think coming. Get on the bikes and we'll double the four of yuh down to the shed."

"Yeah, get on the bars of these bikes and no tricks," said Lynch.

"Oh boy, oh boy," squeaked Peachy. "C'mon, c'mon. I've never seen a sheila's—"

"Shut up, Peachy," said Lynch. "If you don't shut up, you won't get a turn."

172

"Oh, Vic," said Peachy. "Please, Vic, yuh wouldn't do that would yuh, Vic, Vic?"

It seemed to me he was on the verge of tears.

"Get on those grids and hurry up," snapped Lynch.

"You get on the bar of my bike, Prudence," said D'Arcy Anderson, softly. He put his arm around her. I hit him on the nose with everything I had and he sat down hard. I had knocked someone down. I could hardly credit it. I had actually knocked someone down. Just like a film-star in a serial picture.

"By hell!" yelled Skin Hughson, making a grab for me and I hit him too. Then I hacked his shins and hit him again. Down he went. Prudence pushed Lynch and he tripped over Hughson. As Lynch fell he barged over one of his henchmen, who in turn fell over a bicycle. The whole row of bicycles ranged along the kerb crashed to the road one after the other. I heard a smack beside me and there was Clem Walker lying on his face, neatly tripped by Les. Les put the boot in hard and then off he went after Prudence and Angela, already scuttling for safety. Someone dived and tried to collar me low, but they misjudged and stopped a kick in the face. Like the wind the four of us raced along the main street of Klynham.

We ran the whole length of the street before we stopped outside the White Hart. There were some people hanging around the doorway and we felt safe here. To our dismay, Angela was not with us. She had been headed off by a Lynchite on a bicycle.

To dodge her pursuer, Angela had cut across the road to dive down the alley between Charlie Dabney's and the Federal Hotel, but two other Lynchites on flying bicycles had reached the mouth of the alley first. They dismounted and grabbed her. Angela wriggled like an eel and, as she wrenched away, we heard the rip of her frock, clear to where we were standing. They grabbed her again, and

173

again she wrenched herself loose. This time the poor kid lost her frock altogether.

The Lynchites stood around Angela immobilized by the spectacle of their prey clad only in stockings, knickers and singlet. Suddenly Angela darted up the alley and out of sight. With a whoop the Lynchites set off in pursuit, leaving one of their bicycles propped against the hotel and the others lying on the footpath.

"The dirty swine," yelled Prudence. "The dirty pack uv barstids."

I cannot say just how much of the events across the road had been witnessed by the three or four men standing around, but when Prudence yelled at them to come and help, they followed us willingly enough, though not at top speed. I heard them laughing among themselves.

"Hurry, hurry," cried Prudence.

Peachy Blair was coming back down the alley but, when he saw the gang of us arrive, he fled up it again and vanished around the bend.

We hunted everywhere, even called out from the top of the quarry. It gives me the creeps remembering how we called out "Angela! Angela!" and the echo in the quarry answering, *Angela! Angela!*

It is quite probable that she heard our hallooing, but was either too ashamed to emerge, or did not recognize our voices. Just exactly where she was hiding we were never to know.

Prudence was still white and shaking with rage when the three of us arrived at our place. Prudence was carrying Angela's torn gym frock, which she had picked off the footpath. With a rock she had started in to smash up the Lynchites' bicycles, but one of the men who had come to our assistance had restrained her. Quietly Les and I had put our shoes through a few wheel spokes and smashed a headlight. War had been declared.

Prudence changed and said she was going to Angela's

place. Les and I went with her. Angela had not arrived. We told her father what had happened. Grim faced, he went back into the Potroz' little cottage, got his hat and a big walking stick and away we went, ducking under an arch of rambler roses half-way along the narrow, dirt path. Again we searched the alleyway and peered into the quarry.

"Angela! Angela!" called Mr Potroz.

Angela! Angela! the echo answered.

It was getting gloomy and, without Mr Potroz, Les and I would have lacked the courage to investigate. The grim windows of the Dabney chapel presided over the scene. Prudence shuddered.

"Well," said Mr Potroz, "there's only one thing to do. The police. That's what the police are for. If anything has happened to Pet, I'll take the skin off those louts, myself. I'll beat them black and blue."

Happily we followed him. When we arrived at the police station, Prudence plumped for waiting outside.

"No, no, Prudence, come on in," said Mr Potroz. "We want to know all we can about this. I'll tell you what one of us could do, and that's just run home and see if Angela has turned up."

"I will," said Les.

We told the whole story to the sergeant. While we were in the office gabbling it all out, Len Ramsbottom arrived. He managed not to look at Prudence while the sergeant relayed the story to him.

Les arrived, puffed out. Angela was not home.

"I don't like this," said Mr Potroz. "It's getting late, I don't like this a bit."

"Take the big car," said the sergeant. "I'll ring Syd to pop back and take station duty and I'll come myself."

Having the sergeant with us and all must have given Mr Lynch a nasty turn when he answered the door. He overlooked asking us inside. He came back and said,

"According to Victor he knows nothing about it. Some of his friends apparently—"

"I want to see the boy himself," snapped the sergeant, who was a tough character. "I don't want to hear the cock-and-bull stories he tells you. Bring him out."

In the dusk, Prudence and Les and I nudged each other gleefully.

Victor Lynch looked about as much like an all-powerful gangleader tonight as a duckling looks like a black hawk. However, he stuck to his story. He admitted bailing us up in the main street "for a joke" but after that he had come straight home, he averred.

We piled into the Hudson sedan again and continued our inquiries.

Peachy Blair, Skin Hughson and Don Butcher all told the same story. They admitted chasing Angela "for a joke" but said she had ducked them somehow, down the alley-way. Only the presence of the police, in my opinion, stopped Mr Potroz from waling into them with his walking stick.

As we climbed into the Hudson, Les had a rush of brains to the head. "What about the shed?" he cried. "That's where they said they were gunna take us."

Fitzherbert's old shed looked sinister and forbidding. In the car Prudence took my hand.

"You wait there," the sergeant said roughly to us youngsters when we were half-way up the path. Mr Potroz groaned. They shone their torches around inside the shed while we waited in fear and trembling. They found nothing.

"Do you think there's any chance she might be home by now?" we heard Mr Potroz say to the sergeant and Len Ramsbottom as they came down the path to where we were standing.

"We'll go round and see," said the sergeant. "I hope she is."

"My God, so do I. My God, where could she be? Poor little Pet."

I feel positive it is no exaggeration to say that, if any of us had suffered from a weak heart, he or she would have been in extreme danger at that moment of passing in their cheques. I had a heart like a Leyland ten-tonner, but all the same its timing gear slipped badly for a moment or two. There wafted to us from somewhere behind the shed the most blood-curdling wail to ever assail my ear-drums. Then it came again, even more eerie and terrifying than before. Prudence took off for the car with a cry of terror.

"Look after Pru," I said and bolted after the cops, whose torches were already picking a way across the meadow towards the pine belt. The scream came again. It seemed like the sobbing rising and falling wail of an un-hinged mind. Right then my blood would have delighted a vampire who preferred his on the rocks.

"Wait for me, wait for me," I heard Prudence moaning, and I waited while Les and my sister floundered through the long grass to where I was standing. We could see the torchlights picking around among the trees of the orchard. The police and Mr Potroz had found the stile and used it. The shuddering scream sounded again and we hung onto each other. We were all shivering.

"It's up at the big house," said Les. "It's Madam Drac, gone right off her crumpet at last."

"Look! Look!" said Prudence, pointing. The sneering, omniscient moonlight framed her upturned face, a portrait of anyone but Prudence.

"Fire!" said Les.

What we had taken to be drifting cloud against the moon was now plainly smoke. It was tinged with red and, as we listened, we heard the ominous crackle of flame devouring the ancient timber. In the sudden, unholy glare, the pines, prisoners of their own mother, stood aghast.

A torch played on our eyes and Len Ramsbottom came blundering down the slope on top of us.

"Into the car," he snapped. "All of you. Quick now."

He let the clutch in and accelerated so violently we were pitched back into the seat squabs. It was a blind street and the way he spun the car around won my admiration. It was such a big, long car, with such a clumsy lock, we only just made it. Half the width of the tyres on my side— repeat, *my* side—must have been over the deep ditch. I had clambered into the front seat. First I was pitched against the door I had just slammed, and then over I went against the driver's mighty bicep. Gravel flew and the motor roared. The bonnet alone looked bigger than Len's little Austin seven tourer. Around the bend we howled on two wheels—my side again, of course. The old car was not equipped with a Klaxon, but, with Len's elbow clamped hard on the horn button, emitted a fearsome and continuous *ger-oogah*, *ger-oogah* sound. We rocked along the straight like a berserk monster. We rose and fell over the crest of a short but steep hill and swooped down on a sharp bend at an impossible speed.

Never ask me how we got around into that lane.

There was no room for two cars to pass without mounting one of the dirt footpaths at the side, so that is precisely what we did, at sixty miles an hour, to hurtle past a preposterously tall old model T Ford chugging along with the Rev. Higgins at the wheel. I hope and trust he was at his most resilient. I was scared stiff as we whipped along the narrow, winding lane, my eyes glued to the circular glass dial of the temperature gauge, perched up like a mascot at the end of the long, shuddering bonnet. I had to spin around and cling on to the back of the seat as the next corner swept up to meet us and I saw Prudence pitch clear across the back seat on top of Les. Never again was I to sneer at young Constable Ramsbottom. That old Huddy had been designed to glide along, while some very

sedate citizens reclined on velvet and surveyed the land-
scape through lorgnettes, and now here she was lurching
around the bends as if all the devils in hell were an inch
behind the exhaust pipe. Any loiterers on Klynham's
main street must have gawked that night as we went
scorching past. We lurched and skidded to a standstill
outside the lofty shed, which had once been stables, but
now housed the fire-brigade.

Les leaned over from the back seat and breathed heavily
and hotly down my neck.

"Boy," he said. "What a night! This is the real thing.
This has got 'The Fire God's Treasure' stuffed all along
the line."

The Dennis lumbered out on to the road, belching
smoke out of its exhaust. Len turned the police car
around.

"Now Oi want you young people to stay in the car," he
said. "No running around and getting in heverybody's
road. We still haven't found the girl Potroz and we won't
be staying at the fire very long, so stay right where you are
in the car."

Shame on us, we had all but forgotten Angela. This
time Len drove to the front of the old mansion. We wasted
no time, but, compared to the first ride, it was like getting
off the chair-o-plane and onto the merry-go-round. Fitzherbert Street was already jammed with sightseers.

"Confounded idiots," muttered our driver, blasting his
way through the excited throng which swarmed across the
road.

"Now, stay in the car," was his final injunction, as he
slammed his door and strode off in the direction of the
blazing building. We obeyed him, although we were as
fidgety as if we were in a dentist's waiting-room. Next
thing, we were unceremoniously evicted from the car by
the sergeant. As we clambered out we saw, to our horror,
Len Ramsbottom and Mr Potroz approaching with Miss

Fitzherbert held firmly between them. Her head was flung back, the long scrawny throat arched back, her mouth foaming. The glimpse I had of her eyes as they bundled her into the car was to haunt my dreams for many years.

"Gee zuz," said Les.

"Hold on, Mr Potroz," said Len Ramsbottom. "We won't be long."

The police car backed around and drove off through the excited mob, leaving Mr Potroz with us. Speculation was at fever heat among the bystanders.

We heard the muffled crash of heavy beams caving in and a section of roof disappeared down into the shell of smoke and flame that was the great Fitzherbert house.

A man approached Mr Potroz.

"The old girl must have fired the place," Mr Potroz told him. "Channing Fitzherbert has passed away and the shock sent her over the edge. They're getting the old man out now. They should have let him burn down with his castle."

I remember him saying that, and I am in wholehearted agreement. The whole history of Klynham criss-crosses the history of the Fitzherbert family whose might and wealth made the family name a word to conjure with in those parts. No one seemed to know now whether they were millionaires or paupers; they were only shadows glimpsed against the mullioned windows of a mighty house, a house shrouded in decay and mystery. As I said, I agree heartily that the blazing mansion should have been Channing Fitzherbert's funeral pyre. It would have been a fitting end to an epoch but not only that, I have information (or *I think* I have) which would cause a bit of a furore in certain circles. I knew no one would believe me, so I have only mentioned it to one or two. It is my opinion that the impressive tombstone erected to the last of the Fitzherberts in Klynham cemetery marks the grave of a much humbler, if more tragic, traveller through this vale of tears.

Horror upon horror. A clearing was made at the side of the road. A pitifully small bundle, draped in a blanket, was laid reverently down. I realized what was under the blanket; not so Prudence. I was shocked to see her in the forefront of the gazing circle around the little bundle. I made my way to her and took her arm.

"Come away," I said, but I was too late. Some clot flipped back the blanket and we saw the shrunken features and domed, wizened pate of the late master of the house of Fitzherbert. There was a chorus of screams and grunts. Prudence buried her face in my coat.

The police car pulled up beside us.

"Oi ham sorry, Mr Potroz," said Len, "but your daughter has not put in an appearance. It may be advisable to hinstigate a full-scale search."

White as a negro's eyeball, Mr Potroz climbed into the car. We three crawled into the back seat again.

"Nothing can be done here," said Len as we drove away. "Our first duty is to the living." A little further along he said, "Oi am driving you all, with the exception, of course, of Mr Potroz, to your homes where you will all remain. It is late and the toime has come for you to go to bed and leave the work ahead to the police and volun-tuh-heer searchers."

"No, no," wailed Prudence. "I wanna look for Angela. Angela's muh best friend."

"Oi am sorry, Miss Poindexter," said Len heavily. "It does you credit, but home you must go. If your father would care to hoffer his services, it would be happreciated."

So that was that.

In the end Ma got us to bed.

I have never believed in premonitions, or spirit messages or anything, but this is different. I must have heard

181

something, maybe a shout or something drifted up to our corner from the town, a distance not great as the crow flies. Anyway I awoke. I lay in the dark listening. It was not very long before I heard mumbling voices and the board on the veranda creaked. I ran out to the kitchen. The clock on the mantelpiece said twenty minutes past three. Pop and Herbert entered the kitchen and stood like waxen dummies, staring at me. They looked dreadful. Ma came from behind me and next came Prudence, both triumphant over the shapelessness of their nightgowns, the one so indomitable, the one so svelte.

"Well," Ma demanded. "Have you found Angela?"

Pop nodded and sat down and put his head in his hands.

"She's dead," Herbert blurted, his eyes starting out of his head. "Murdered. Strangled. Raped."

Chapter Seventeen

B LACK SUNDAY.
 The murdering and raping of Angela Potroz froze
Klynham in its tracks. The grief of her family slit the
tongue of every busybody. The very clouds in the sky
were sombre. Prudence cut the top off a boiled egg and
then collapsed weeping. Herbert and Pop sat on the back
steps. Ma, grim-faced, drank a lot of tea. Dolly and Monica
played quietly with a rag doll. Les and I crouched down by
the rhubarb. Who? Who? Who?

Dear, pretty Angela with her heart of gold that would
tick no more. No key known to wind her up again. The
recollection of wishing to kiss Angela distressed me. That
my shell could have ever harboured even a distant cousin
of the frenzy which had raged in some murderous fiend
seemed unbelievable. Les and I had very little to say. The
memory of a thousand conversations about sex hung over
us like a pall. We had found and discussed with great ani-
mation a beautiful flower in a beautiful garden and now
its stench had knocked us flat.

Drawn by the same macabre curiosity which affected
everyone in the community as the moon controls the tide,
Pop and Herbert and Les and I made our way to join the
silent, horrified gathering outside Charlie Dabney's premises and the Federal Hotel. The main street was jammed
with groups of people who had made their pilgrimage up
to the alleyway and returned to the main street again. All

183

the back alleys behind the shops were thronged by grim-faced, watching people. The track down to the quarry was roped off. There was an out-of-town police car parked in the alley between the funeral parlour and the high fence along the backyard of the hotel. Nobody wanted to appear interested in cars at a time like this, but all the men and quite a few of the women were unable to resist peering into and around the strange police car. It was an Airflow Chrysler, the first anyone in Klynham had ever seen.

Les and I were peering through the windows of the car when Len Ramsbottom came up and bade us follow him. The local police car, the big Hudson, was parked in the main street with its motor running. Prudence was sitting in the front seat and a chalk-white Peachy Blair in the back. Les and I climbed in and sat with Peachy Blair.

Mr Lynch was standing on the steps of the police station when we arrived, but no one spoke. Prudence, Les and I were taken into one room, Peachy Blair into another. All the rooms seemed to be busy. Typewriters were tapping and through the doors came the sounds of deep voices.

Len found us seats and left us in the room. We stared at each other. Soon a big man, a city detective, entered and took our statements. He kept them very brief and to the point.

"I want you two to wait outside," he said to Prudence and Les. Now the whole story about how the Lynchites had beaten me up and how they had wanted to bring Prudence to the shed was unfolded in detail. I told the detective all about Don Butcher and Peachy Blair. Although I was scared stiff and my heart thumped, I was sorry when he dismissed me. I felt more important than I had ever felt and, at the same time, more humble.

"I want you to keep this to yourself," the detective told me. "I don't want you going around the town spreading this around. I'll want to see you again later when Detective Inspector Peterjohn arrives."

Following his instructions I told no one except Les and Prudence and, of course, Pop and Herbert and Ma. Ma absolutely gibbered upon finally hearing the truth about how my rib was broken. She put her arms around Prudence and stroked her hair and moaned to herself.

At about three o'clock in the afternoon Len Ramsbottom called for me in the little Austin and I knew I was being taken to meet the great man from the Criminal Investigation Department.

"Who do you think did it, officer?" I asked Len on the way to the police station.

"We'll soon nah-ho," he said. "There isn't much doubt it was one, or even two of those louts. Probably those who tore the kid's frock off. Blair seems to be in the clear, but they tell the same story so far. They won't last long with Detective Inspector Peterjohn, Oi'm telling you."

"That means it was Skin Hughson, or Don Butcher, then," I said. "They're the ones that chased her up the alley with Peachy Blair."

"It isn't conclusive. There is hevidence the actual rape was committed elsewhere and the bah-hody taken to the quarry."

"It could have been any of them, or the lot of them," I breathed. "It could have been Lynch. The dirty sods, the dirty—filthy—"

"We shall soon nah-ho," said Len Ramsbottom.

However, Len Ramsbottom was wrong. The truth was as infuriatingly beyond reach as a word on the tip of the tongue. The cards were face up on the table, but no selection made up a hand. The town crawled with detectives and simmered with fierce speculation, but no one knew anything. Hourly a fresh rumour was launched, only to founder. There was no other topic of conversation, except, perhaps a few digressions on the Fitzherbert fire.

The empty seats of the entire Lynch gang in the classrooms on Monday, when school re-opened after the May vacation, was felt to be sinister and most significant, but in the afternoon they were all occupied, except that of Peachy Blair. A rumour that he had committed suicide by cutting his throat and jumping under a train, and another that he was locked in a cell, wherein he had hung himself, expired with ill grace when teachers at school announced that they thought it better for us all to be told that Peachy was very ill and suffering from nervous prostration. Within the hour he had taken poison and died in the most awful convulsions. On Tuesday he was back at school.

The name Lynch began to have an ominous ring and secondary meaning. People stood in dark groups on corners and in doorways. It was rumoured that a voice had telephoned the police station demanding information. The rapist would never reach the gallows, the anonymous voice asserted. A hooded company, said the voice, would show the police how it should be done. The only substantiation of these exciting rumours was vaguely embarrassing. In a deep drain, outside the farmlet owned by the Dalmation who illicitly distilled the applejack, a local eccentric was discovered, a sack, complete with eyeholes, drawn over his head. He had been in the drain all night.

Tuesday was the day of the funeral. The entire roll-call asked for permission to attend. It was granted to everyone over the second standard. Some said the funeral would be at 11 a.m. Others said it was scheduled for 2 p.m. The headmaster telephoned Charlie Dabney and, on the strength of the answer he was given, the school assembled at 10.45 to march to town. It was an overcast day. The clouds were curtains, not quite drawn close enough together to keep out the odd shaft of sunlight. The shuffling footfalls of the school on the march brought people to their gates and windows.

Prudence was sweeping the footpath outside the Federal

186

Hotel when she saw the procession approaching. She clapped a hand over her mouth and bolted inside, plucking at her apron as she went.

The teachers went around arranging us in a semicircle. The big puddle in the middle of the road mercilessly revealed us as a shock-haired, scraggy bunch. There was a little talk among the pupils, but it soon died away as our eyes became focused on the high bonnet of the vintage Hupmobile hearse, which was backed up the alley by the open doors of the chapel.

Prudence emerged from the Federal wearing an old black overcoat buttoned right up to her neck. She soon picked me out and came up to me.

"I thought it wuz this afternoon," she muttered. "They told me it wuz this afternoon. I thought this wuz Mr Fitzherbert's funeral until I saw all you kids coming."

"No, it's at eleven," I said.

"I want tuh see Angela."

"Don't be silly," I said, patting her arm.

"No, but I want tuh see her," she said. "They wouldn't let me come and see her before, but I think I should before it's too late. I think Angela would want me tuh see her."

"Where's Ma and Pop?" I muttered.

"It's that ole fool, Charlie Dabney," said Prudence. "He's messed everything up."

"Maybe they're up at the service in the chapel," I suggested.

"C'mon," said Prudence and, catching me by the wrist, pulled me after her. The teachers said nothing as we crossed the road and went up the alley. We stopped dead when Uncle Athol in a moth-eaten dark suit and bowler hat came out of the chapel and climbed into the hearse.

"We're too late," I said. A very old, very frail and slightly mad-looking little woman approached Prudence

187

and me, and, when she saw we were holding hands, she began to cry.

"So beautiful," she said. "So very, very beautiful. Never be afraid of death, my dear littul boy and girl. All sorrow and evil shall be washed away by the angels. All the suffering of life is transformed into beauty. It is ten years since I saw Channing in his misery and suffering, but death has made him as sweet and beautiful as a littul girl."

She made a series of passes at us as if she were blessing us and sprinkling us with holy water.

"Death is beautiful," she said. "Channing, in death, is as beautiful as a littul girl. In his casket he looked like an angel. All night I have seen his face as serene and lovely as a littul girl's."

"We're gunna get run over," I said sharply. Charlie Dabney in frock coat and top hat was rolling sedately (if it is possible to roll sedately on tubby, brandy-happy legs) down the alley towards us and the hearse was following him silently. The alley sloped to the street and Uncle Athol, perched at the wheel, was just allowing the hearse to coast. Whenever the high prow of the old Hupmobile seemed just on the point of flattening Charlie, walking in front with as much dignity as his small, rotund body could muster, the vehicle braked sharply. As soon as Charlie had a few yards start the hearse began to roll again.

"Look out," said Prudence, and took the little old lady by the arm. Between us we hustled her down to the street. A moment later Charlie Dabney staggered past us and fell on his knees. It was easy to guess that Uncle Athol had lost his footing on the brake and caught his employer a nasty clip from behind. A loud snigger flitted through the ranks of assembled schoolchildren.

One of the teachers helped old Charlie Dabney to his feet. One of the pupils retrieved the top hat, put it on for a fleeting instant, and then returned it. The snigger was a guffaw this time. While the mortician adjusted the hat on his head the self-starter of the hearse whirred feebly. Charlie stood to attention, back to the hearse, and then walked slowly forwards. The self-starter continued to whirr. Charlie Dabney was quite a long way down the street before someone stopped him. The teachers, very red in the face, were doing their best to control their hysterical wards. I saw Miss McGlashan, our art teacher, stuff a little handkerchief into her mouth.

When Charlie Dabney was brought back he went around to the cab of the hearse. Uncle Athol handed him a crank-handle through the window. Charlie bestowed on his driver a look designed to burn him to a cinder, then walked around the bonnet looking about him at his audience, and simpering apologetically.

First pull of the crank and the motor started, but the hearse was in gear and shot forward. Charlie vanished under the front fender and the top hat flew away on its travels again. By this time no attempt was being made to control the convulsions of the school. The headmaster had covered his eyes. Without warning, Miss McGlashan departed.

Charlie was extricated from under the hearse and dusted down. Someone put the top hat back on his head at a rakish angle.

Uncle Athol tried the starter again and this time the motor caught. The racket the motor kicked up was a great relief to those who were painfully bottling up their mirth. It began to appear that the disgraceful episode was ended and that the funeral would now proceed with some pretence of dignity, but right then one of the teachers came out of the alley and approached the headmaster. The news flew around like a stick in a party game. It was the wrong funeral. The school had lined up to watch the hilarious last ride of Channing Fitzherbert.

"I am unable to find it in my heart," the headmaster

said in his address to the school after lunch, "to punish anyone for their behaviour this morning. Laughter is a natural function and I think that not only the pupils, but the staff also found some of the mishaps this morning uncontrollably diverting. We can only be thankful that it was the funeral of an old man and that it was not attended by any of his kith and kin. This afternoon Angela is leaving us forever. I know we all loved Angela. Her heart-broken parents will be present and I want all of you to understand quite clearly that no matter what may eventuate—I repeat, *no matter what*, anyone guilty of laughter will be severely punished."

Miss McGlashan appeared to be chewing her cud. That handkerchief was surely getting a thrashing.

But no one laughed when we assembled outside Charlie Dabney's at two o'clock. The sight of Mr and Mrs Potroz would have robbed any spectacle of humour. Prudence was with them, openly weeping, and soon all the girls were weeping too. I was not far off it myself. It was while I was standing there that I overheard a conversation which gave me a nasty turn. Two relatives of the Potroz' were standing behind me.

"My God," said one of them, "hanging's too good for this swine. I'd gouge his eyes out. I'd roast the bastard alive. God Almighty, it makes you wonder if there is a God. When I saw her face in her box there, I nearly fainted."

"So did I," said the other voice. "One glimpse was enough for me, by God. He musta torn her to bits. He musta torn her hair out. Hell! it doesn't stand thinking about."

No wonder, I thought, they refused to let Prudence see poor Angela. I felt sick right through.

"Christ," said the first voice, "I can't credit some kid did anything like that. It's the work of a fiend. I remember her as such a pretty little thing and Godstruth lying there,

190

her face looked like an old man about eighty. She musta gone through hell."

Everyone was moving away from the hearse, but I stood stock-still. Charlie Dabney was making no attempt this afternoon to walk in front of the hearse, but was propped up in the cab with Uncle Athol.

Probably can't walk by this time, I thought bitterly; but, in the main, my mind was busy piecing the odd scraps of overheard conversation together. First, the old lady this morning had said Channing Fitzherbert had looked in death as beautiful as a little girl, and now I had heard Angela's appearance described as that of an old man. With all her hair torn out. It added up, by God, it added up. As I moved off after the hearse I wondered wildly if perhaps my homage was not being paid to old Channing Fitzherbert, after all.

That Angela's mother was nearly out of her mind with grief was not only a local topic, but also obvious to all with eyes to see. In his misery and concern, it was more than probable that Mr Potroz had left final arrangements in the numb hands of Charlie Dabney, himself, in person.

There was no gauging the drunken folly of Charlie Dabney and his lieutenant, Uncle Athol. If the coffins had been confused in the chapel and relatives conducted to and shown the wrong corpse perhaps the farce had been carried out to the bitter end. There was no telling now; and I knew, right then, trudging along in silence, there never would be an answer.

I will confess that I shied at including this account of that Tuesday in my little narrative, as I feel it to be in the worst taste. On the other hand, its omission would have left me feeling guilty of withholding some aspects of Klynham's dark hour and, when all is said and done, it is to these moments in the town's history my recording pen has inexorably led me.

The Hupmobile hearse never reached the graveside.

With a grinding crash it collided with the left-hand pillar of the great ornamental stone gates of the cemetery. The pall-bearers had a long walk. Charlie Dabney and Uncle Athol were conspicuous by their absence at the graveside, too. They slumbered peacefully in the cab of the wrecked Hupmobile.

So it came to pass that the next court day at Klynham was not marked by any sensational unmasking or preliminary trial of Angela's killer, but only by the usual crop of people who had ridden bicycles without lights, and Uncle Athol who was charged with being drunk-in-charge and in consequence lost his driving licence for twelve months. The shame of it all.

Chapter Eighteen

D ETECTIVE INSPECTOR PETER JOHN became a familiar
figure around Klynham, as familiar as the posters on
the corrugated-iron walls of the cinema for "Palmy Days"
and nearly as tattered. The Airflow Chrysler came and
went. Between police and reporters it was as if Klynham
had become a tourist resort. The papers—city papers and
weeklies—were beginning to clamour for retribution.
"What were the police doing?" they asked. It was a ques-
tion we were all asking.

Les and I were anxious to play detective, but we lacked
the nerve to go down into the quarry. We ventured down
one afternoon when there were a few other people poking
around and we had the actual spot, where Angela's body
was found, pointed out to us; but, after that, whenever we
returned it was a dark deserted place, a place of horror,
and, as I said, our nerve failed us.

There was nothing superficial about the grief of Prudence. Like Rachel she mourned and would not be com-
forted. She went daily with flowers to the cemetery and it
was this more than anything, I think, which kept my trap
closed concerning my deep suspicion about which grave
harboured who.

For the first time since Pop and Ma had married, we
were shot of Uncle Athol. Prudence saw him each day,
working as she still was at the Federal, for Uncle Athol

had found himself living quarters somewhere in the rambling building which belonged to Charlie Dabney and such time as he did not spend there, he spent leaning over the bar in the hotel.

There was no actual romance springing up between Les and Prudence, but at least he saw more of her now than any of her other admirers. The others still hung around of course, in fact, in greater numbers and with more persistence than heretofore, but Prudence seemed to have no patience with them. Les and Prudence and I spent quiet evenings at home, talking around the fire and making up a scrapbook. We went to the flicks together and on Friday nights we tried to roller skate. This was a new craze in Klynham, started by the proprietor of a bicycle shop who had rented an old hall, was hiring out skates and charging sixpence for admission.

It was just a month after the murder of Angela when Les and I, one Friday night, called for Prudence at the Federal Hotel to take her skating and were told she was not there. We were known at the pub by now and had gone straight down to the kitchen. The cook told us Prudence must have gone.

"I've just been upstairs," she said, "and she's not there. She was hanging out clothes on the annexe veranda line after tea, and I haven't seen her since." She looked out the kitchen window. "She's not out there now."

Les and I looked out at the backyard but it was dark and deserted. I could see the white, ghostly shapes of sheets and pillow slips hanging from the clothesline on the annexe veranda.

"We're running a bit late, Neddy," said Les. "Maybe she's gone down to the skating."

We stood in the front doorway of the hotel for a few minutes, looking up and down the main street and it was while we were there that we saw Herbert and Uncle

Athol go in through the front door of Charlie Dabney's furniture shop.

"That brother of yours is getting to be nearly as big a hophead as yer uncle," observed Les. "C'mon, let's get along down."

The first people to pounce on us at the skating were the Headly sisters, Marjorie and Beth. They were well-known hard cases in Klynham, short-skirted, gum-chewing, full of fun, precocious. They must have had Les and me marked down, we never had a chance. We forgot all about Prudence. We walked the sisters home after the skating, both of us quite incoherent and with our hearts pounding deliriously. At last we had graduated from the outside-looking-in class. The sisters were far from incoherent. When they were not smooging up to us and teasing us for being shy they danced along the narrow footpath and sang scatty songs.

> He doesn't look like much of a lover
> > But cha don't judge a book by its cover.
> In a taxi-cab—hmm hmm
> > Or in a Morris chair—hmm hmm
> Yoo-hoo-ud be surprised.

At the garden gate we received the most wonderful kiss of all—the first. Not only that, but Beth stuck her tongue in my mouth. I thought it was her chewing-gum at first. Marjorie had done the same to Les, he told me.

"Looks to me," he said, as we walked back, "that these two sheilas are gunna be the ones to learn all about you-know with."

"I wonder what it is like?" he said, just before we parted at the corner.

"What?" I asked.

"You-know," he said.

"Accordin' to Herbert," I told him, "it's like bluebirds flyin' outa yuh backside."

195

"Is that really what Herbert said?" Les seemed greatly impressed. I know now that these were not my big brother's own words at all, but those of some mute, inglorious Milton; in fact, I knew then, but, because it seemed to put Herbert up a peg or two in Les's eyes, I let it ride. After all blood is thicker than water.

Chapter Nineteen

"ZIZ FLUSH," said Charlie Dabney. "Flush beats straight every friggin' time. Great Scott, Athol, you old scoundrel, I've headed you off you ole reprobate."

"Ha, ha," said Uncle Athol. "Not friggin' flush at*tall*, not even hand of any sort, four friggin' hearts anna diamond, not even a friggin' pair."

"Well, I'll be frigged."

"And I'll tell *you* something, Athol," said Herbert. "Hate to menshun this and all that, but nine, ten, Jack, King, ace, aren't friggin' straight either. Where's friggin' Queen?"

Charlie Dabney cackled long and loud as Uncle Athol examined his cards. He brushed a tear from his eye. "Great Scott, never laughed so much in all muh friggin' life. Haftu have a lil' drink on that. Liesh won't go out all night. No flush, no straight, wouldn't read about it. Strordinary affair." He groped around for the brandy bottle. He looked behind the box he was sitting on.

"Athol," said Charlie, sternly, "where's the brandy? Have you flogged my brandy bottle, you old rapscallion?"

"Havva beer," said Herbert.

"Stick it," said Charlie. "Brandy bottles vanishing rightnleft lately 'round here. Very mysterious. Maybe not so friggin' mysterious after all. Maybe perfectly logical explainaesh. Same explainaesh as food vanishing rightnleft all the time. Same explainaesh as cigarette lighter vanishing. Very simple, logical explainaesh. Traitor in camp. Viper in bosom. Great Scott, biting the hand that rocks the cradle."

"Just what—"

"Bottle was over there a minute ago," said Herbert. "Saw it muhself. Yuh left it on that bench there. No one's been near that bench."

"Perfectly simple, logical explainaesh. See it all now. Viper in bosom. Name of viper, Athol Claude friggin' Cudby."

"I beg your bloody, friggin' pardon," said Uncle Athol, haughtily.

"Just wait a minute," said Herbert, arising somewhat unsteadily from the box he was sitting on.

"I'll have you know—"

"Perfectly simple, logical—"

"Shurrup," hissed Herbert. He held up his hand for silence.

"Accuse me of friggin' stealing would—"

"Perfectly straiford, simple, logical—"

"Shrrup," hissed Herbert. He began to tip-toe away on a tour of inspection of the vast, shadowed room. The only light came from a very tiny electric globe suspended by a flex and hanging very low above the scattered playing cards.

Herbert told me that he now received the biggest fright of his whole life. I am sure I am the only person he ever confided in. He had a very good reason for this reticence, i.e. the shadow of the gallows.

Herbert tip-toed around the end of a great pile of old furniture and timber and came face to face with Salter the Sensational. His heart, as near as dammit, stopped.

"There's your thief," he yelled, staggering back. "There he is. There he is."

Salter advanced, brandy bottle in hand. Herbert backed away.

"Great Scott," babbled Charlie Dabney. "You, you villain. Thought you'd robbed my till and decamped weeks ago, you distardly bastard. All the time still here, robbing ole Charlie, causing trouble between me and dear ole frien' like Athol. Cause of wild accusaesh against dear ole frien'. Nev' forgive, nev' forgive."

"Qui' awright, Charlie, qui' awright, forget whole affair, qui' understan'—"

"Very noble, Athol, heart of gold, episode definitely not closed. Too much altogether. Ring police immediately. Ring friggin' police. Get Smith, hah."

In high dudgeon, Charlie Dabney set off for his little office, but he covered very little distance before Salter had him by the throat. He arched the fat, little undertaker back and sank his thumbs deep into the jugular vein. It would have been all up with Charlie in one minute flat, but Uncle Athol and Herbert between them managed to tear Salter loose. At close range he stunk like a polecat.

Purple in the face, Charlie fell to the floor. Salter felled Uncle Athol with a murderous blow. Herbert retreated. Snarling like a tiger, Salter began to stalk him. Herbert backed into the pile of timber and, reaching behind him, tried to wrench loose a plank. Salter stopped and groped under his armpit. His hand emerged empty, but not a muscle of his freak-ugly face twitched. He charged and pounced. Only mad terror gave Herbert the strength to wield the plank and even with this boost he only swung it high enough to wipe Salter's long, flying legs from underneath him. Salter's temple hit the edge of a coffin lid, jammed firm in the pile of timber. He lay still.

Herbert helped his uncle to his feet. They both lifted up Charlie Dabney and lowered him into a sitting position on a box.

"I've knocked the bastard out," said Herbert. "We

better tie him up or something. This guy is dangerous."

Uncle Athol had found and picked up the brandy bottle. They all had a suck at it.

"Great Scott," said Charlie Dabney, massaging his throat. "Nearly lost my ticket for soup that trip. What a scoundrel! Gimme another drink and I'll ring the jondomerohso. Ring Smith, hah."

"Yuh better hurry," said Herbert, eyeing the recumbent form of Salter the Sensational.

Uncle Athol went over and examined Salter. After a while he turned around, cold sober, and said, "There isn't any hurry."

Chapter Twenty

I SLEPT BLISSFULLY all night, emotionally intoxicated with a few kisses and Beth Headly poking her tongue down my throat. I was ever a person of simple tastes.

Herbert arrived home hours later than usual, but his arrival did not awaken me. In the morning I woke him up, not intentionally, but by roaming the sunlit bedroom singing, "There's a War in Abyssinia, Wontcha Come. Go Getcha Peanuts andya Gun", to the tune of "Roll Along Covered Wagon, Roll Along".

Herbert rolled over and yawned languorously. Then he sat bolt upright. Even his hair stood up on end.

"What's wrong?" I queried.

"Whas wrong?" repeated Herbert. "Jesus, did you say whas wrong?"

"That's what I said, man."

"Oh my God," said Herbert. He tottered across the room, smacking his forehead.

"Well, what is wrong?"

"Nothin'," he muttered. "Nothin'. Gotta lot to do, thas all. Gotta get the truck off Pop and pick up some junk from a joker's place. Promised I'd run it down to the tip."

"Well, it's early yet."

"Promised I'd be early. Hell! Where's muh shirt? Where's muh fags?"

"Yuh better cut out smoking," I told him. "You're shaking like an aspro leaf."

When I got out to the washhouse, Herbert was leaning over one of the tubs being sick.

"Thas booze for you," I jeered. "Yuh better lay off the booze, as well as smokes, or yuh just gunna be Uncle Athol the second."

"Shut up, willyuh!" Herbert screamed at me.

"I'm sorry, kid," he said a moment later. He was sweating like a pig. He went out of the washhouse and I shrugged my shoulders. He poked his head back in and said, "Tell Pop I'm taking the Dennis to pick up a load. Tell 'im I'll be back before any time at all to speak of."

When I came out on the veranda he was cranking the truck. Every two or three spins he had a rest and leaned on the radiator. As I went inside, the old girl fired.

"You're up early," said Ma to me as I entered the kitchen. "Whas got into everybody? Herbert out of bed at the crack of dawn. Prudence gone—"

"When did she go?" I asked.

"I dunno, I didn't see her. But she's gone."

"Oh." That was all I said, but I went cold from head to toe. Oh no, please God, not Prudence.

"Yuh want some porridge?" Ma asked.

"I'll have some soon," I said. "Yes, soon. I'll nip down the street first."

"Look Eddy," said Ma, "venturing forth on an empty stomach is just about the surest way in thuh world to pick up every germ known to science, and then some. The atmosphere we breathe aboundinates in the vilest germs, as Grandma Cudby would be the first to tell yuh, and nothing looks like a good landing place to the above-average germ more than an empty gutz at the crack uv dawn."

"See yuh," I muttered. I ran all the way to the Federal. Prudence had not put in an appearance. None of the kitchen staff had seen her. They looked at me curiously. Out on the street I paced up and down biting my nails.

To my surprise I saw our old Dennis parked up the alley-way by Dabney's chapel. I glimpsed Herbert and Uncle Athol. They seemed to be loading the tray with a lot of old timber and junk. I figured that in an old building like Dabney's there would be enough junk to sink a boat. I wondered if Herbert was putting one across Pop. Probably owed more money, I thought. To hell with him anyway! I began to jog-trot in the direction of the police station. Sun before seven, I thought crazily, rain before eleven. Great isolated drops of rain were falling, hitting me on the head hard, thudding into the ground around me as I jog-trotted. The sky was greying over. The huge raindrops were like a pup's pawmarks. I had an all-alone, desperate, melancholy feeling. I was incapable of running any faster, or doing anything more than just jog-trot. My heart thumped louder than my feet. Sun before seven, sun before seven.

Len Ramsbottom, heading for the police station also, pulled up just ahead of me out on the road. Through a hole in a celluloid side-curtain of the Austin, I gabbled my fears out to him.

"Get in," he snapped.

As we puttered out on to the main street our old Dennis, its radiator steaming, chugged past in the op-posite direction. Herbert was driving. It looked like Charlie Dabney's fat face by Herbert's shoulder and, I guessed, the third figure in the cab was that of Uncle Athol. It was hard to see clearly in the driving rain, but the three of them looked miserable and unusually pale, almost grey. They were staring straight ahead with set faces.

Constable Len Ramsbottom and I stood out in the slashing rain in the middle of the backyard of the Federal Hotel and stared around hopelessly at the big oil-drums, which served for trash-cans, and the heaps of empty crates and casks. Everywhere the raindrops spurted and bounced, and everything (us included) was sodden wet. Faces, masked by windows and the curtains of upstairs rooms, watched us.

We had explored every inch of the yard. We had prowled along the annexe veranda, ducking under the sheets and pillow slips which Prudence had pegged on the line. We had examined all the rooms opening off the veranda, turning everything over, even looking under the tubs in the washhouse. It was while we were in the washhouse that I must have seen it first, but my meter had failed to register. I must have thought it was a belt-buckle or something of that nature.

By now, the early daylight had been so throttled by the evil clouds that we could have been abroad in a winter's dusk. I looked· up wretchedly at the tall young policeman's face and he looked down just as wretchedly into mine.

"Go up on the veranda outa the rain, Neddy," he said. "Oi won't be long." He removed an improvised latch, a short length of 3 x 2 timber, and opened an iron gate in the high fence. It opened up on the alley between the hotel and the funeral parlour. Now I knew where he was going. The quarry! Oh no, please God! I stood in the rain paralysed by the realization of what the simple words "too late" could mean.

"We'll fa-hind her," Len Ramsbottom had said to me, as we had driven along the street in his little car. "We'll pull this town apart, board by board, stone by stone, until we do."

"Ber-rick by ber-rick," he had added, as we picked up steam. My eyes had glittered when I heard him say these things.

I thought now: bone by bone. The thought was only a flick, but the drenching rain was neither wet nor cold enough to instantly revive me.

The formless faces in the Federal were still watching,

so the nape of my neck told me. My mind moved in ever diminishing, concentric circles until finally the yard and the annexe and the rain and the piece of loose iron banging on a roof all faded from me and I could only see one small article, a piece of black cloth. Like a mad thing, I rushed into the washhouse. The washhouse was frighteningly dark and empty. There it was on the floor. Gingerly I picked it up. A shiver zig-zagged up my spine.

"Len!" I screamed. "Len! Len! Len!"

He met me at the top of the track down to the quarry.

"Salter the Sensational," I babbled. "It's his bow tie. It's him that musta killed Angela. It's him that's killed Prudence. He hid in a shed in Smythe Street and waited for her one night, she told me. Because we laughed at him. He's killed her! He's killed her—"

Len began to run back down into the quarry. He stopped and looked back at me. He looked demented.

"Charlie Dabney," I yelled above the rain. "He'll know where to find him."

He blundered past me like a buffalo. When he started to kick in the chapel doors, I tugged at his arm.

"He's in our truck," I panted. "Just as we came along they drove away with a load of junk heaped on our truck —Uncle Athol and Herbert and Mr Dabney. They're headed for the dump."

"The dump?" said Len, stupidly. He had already kicked one panel of the stout door clean out. It was inch-thick, kauri timber. He must have had a foot like a battle-axe.

"The rubbish tip," I howled, gnawing at my knuckles. "Let's catch him up and find out where Salter is."

We ran for the Austin.

It was uphill to the rubbish tip and the little car made hard work of the trip. I leaned forward as if to help the motor. My fist was jammed in my mouth.

"Oi didn't believe her," groaned Len. "Jesus forgive me. Oi didn't believe her."

So great was my horror of rats that I had resolved never again to revisit the tip. It was considered to be an honour to be invited by older boys, air-rifle owners, to accompany them to the tip on a rat-shooting expedition, but once had been more than enough for me. The rodent-infested gully, crammed with tins and paper and reeking filth was, for me, the stuff of nightmares. There was no need for me, as we scrambled from the car, to glance at the drunkenly leaning notice to glean what it announced. The signboard slanted at the same 45 degree angle as the driving rain. KLYNHAM BOROUGH RUBBISH TIP. POISON LAID FOR RATS.

Our old Dennis tip-truck, resembling, beneath this lowering sky, some armoured, malevolent reptile of the past, was backed up to the gully and a great assortment of old timber and boxes and rubbish was noisily cascading off the tilted tray, down into the putrefaction below. The policeman and I ran across the squelching ground. Uncle Athol, Herbert and Charlie Dabney, stood aghast like the skeletons of lightning-devoured trees.

"This Salter," rapped Len. "You know this man, Salter, Mr Dabney. Where is he? Where does he live? Quick now!"

"He's got Prudence," I gabbled. "He killed Angela. It's him, I tell yuh. I found his bow tie. He might have killed Prudence, we gotta find him, we gotta. Prudence hasn't been seen since last night. Where is he?"

Charlie Dabney sank down on the sodden ground. He was soaked through and through and he was ashen faced. "Brandy," he croaked. "Athol, don't leave me to die. Brandy."

"The shop!" Herbert suddenly yelled. "That's where the swine's been hiding. In the shop. Hiding somewhere in Charlie's shop."

Again Len and I ran for the Austin. The little car

turned for town as if it were chasing its tail. We hit every bump over the brow of the hill full steam ahead.

This time Len put his shoulder to the front doors of Dabney's shop. They flew apart with a splintering crack. The very first charge we were in. I followed him into the gloomy shop, rejoicing in his massive strength and giant outline.

"Prudence!" he called. "Come out, Salter! Don't try to escape. Oi'm armed and Oi'll shoot to kill."

We listened. I knew Len carried as many arms as a harbour dredge. I looked over my shoulder as if I were alone in the dark. The plate-glass window rippled with rain and the street beyond was a shadow-show. The door behind us banged brokenly and I jumped in terror. I remembered Prudence running out from the shop the night we had come with Herbert, the night she had reckoned she had seen Salter. I could see her beautiful big eyes bright as stars with fear, and I could hear her husky voice saying "Standing among the *coffins*." I whimpered. To be standing breathing this lily-sick air, in this musty hole among the waxen wreaths in those round glass cases, and to be thinking of lovely, sparkling Prudence, was horrible. Stealthily, Len began to advance. It was all I could make myself do to follow him.

Half-way along a narrow passage was a tiny office with a littered desk and a telephone. An empty brandy bottle stood beside the 'phone. Half a cigar, well chewed, was on the floor. I ran after Len. We were in the big storeroom and cabinet-making shop. My heart nearly stopped as Len pounced forward and tore aside a grey velvet curtain. As a matter of fact, he ripped it beyond repair. We were confronted by a row of brandy bottles on a shelf. We saw the playing cards scattered on the floor. There were empty bottles everywhere.

"Prudence," Len called.

Our only answer was the muffled thunder of rain.

"Prudence," I called. My voice sounded cracked and feeble.

"Prudence!" Len bellowed.

We threw stealth away and began a frantic hunt. Ruthlessly, we tossed coffins over and pushed aside the obsolete furniture which cluttered the dark corners. Cobwebs reached for us. Along the echoing passages we stamped, smashing open creaking doors and peering into junk-stuffed rooms. Dust rose and fell all about us like a ground mist. At the very back, up a few steps, was a particularly horrible and very dark passageway with grime-coated windows, overlooking, I guessed, the quarry. We stopped half-way along. It led nowhere. I stood behind him, sick with hopelessness. As we came back along the passage we stopped dead.

I can still claim my eyes were sharp, although I had missed the knife on our way along the passage. I can plead that the light, meagre as it was, had been against us. I saw the knife in time to prevent me banging my chin into the arm Len threw across the passage. As the building shuddered so did the hilt of the outsize knife, which riveted our vision. It was as if it had just thudded home into the wall above our heads. It was well over even big Len's head and yet, it dawned on us after our first alarm had abated, it had been slammed up there, effortlessly, in passing. Each time the wind, having battled its way through the ranks of driving rain, shook the building, the hilt of the knife quivered realistically. An intrepid cobweb had already staked its claim on the wicked steel.

"Listen!" I hissed. "Listen!" When I heard the stifled whimper again from behind us I had to clutch Len's arm, or I would have fallen.

"Prudence!" he roared.

It is very easy to abandon effort just when triumph is at hand. In our despair, we had very nearly done just that. At the end of the passage was an enormous, ancient, very ornately carved chest of drawers. It had escaped our attention that it was not flush with the end wall and that there were several yards of floor space behind it. My chances of shifting the chest on my own can be discounted, but Len heaved an end up and staggered backwards with it, nearly skittling me in the process. It was as if we had burst into the fetid, bone-strewn lair of a robber dog.

Les pushed me back. "Get out, Neddy," he said. He thought she was dead, and so did I.

"No, no," I whimpered.

Prudence looked terrible lying on her back, half on a ruptured mattress, half on the filthy floor, among cheese rinds, empty fish and meat cans, chop bones, crusts, bottles, cigar ends, rat droppings. She was gagged with a blood-soaked handkerchief. Sash-cord, ripped tight across the gaping wound of her mouth, held the handkerchief in place. Her eyes were glazed with shock and suffering, but it is heavenly to recall the glint of recognition that re-fired them. The first word she mumbled when Len had eased off the gag was "Eddy" and that, also, is heavenly to recall. Then she said, "Len!" He would probably tell you it was the other way around, but she definitely spoke my name first.

"Darling, darling," said Len, as he hacked through the sash-cord with which her arms and legs were trussed. She was scratched and bruised and all her front teeth were missing. She must have fought like a wounded bear. For all the beating she had taken and the hell she had been through, she was still alive and even dressed. Herbert had struck Salter down just in time to prevent his returning, fortified with brandy, to finish off his fell work.

It is ironical that the best thing Herbert ever did in his life has to be kept as dark as a black pudding. Prudence knows, of course, but, girl in a million she is, it has gone no further. Even after all these years, the hunt goes on for Salter the Sensational. I know this is wrong, but what can we do? All I can say is that there could be no more fitting tombstone for that fiend than the rotten, tottering notice board at the Borough Tip.

Klynham has a bush-telegraph that made anything in "The Fire God's Treasure" look ridiculous. It was hard to credit the news could have circulated so quickly. Even Les Wilson was in the crowd that had gathered outside Dabney's shop.

"Well, Neddy," he said to me after we had watched Len Ramsbottom carrying my sister away with her arms around his neck, "I love Prudence so much that I'd uv died if anything had happened to her, but after Marjorie Headly last night sticking her tongue down muh throat and everything, I can't help feeling maybe yuh sister is too old for me. Thas zactly what I thought, Neddy, as soon as Marjorie started this tongue business. I thought, well, Prudence Poindexter is certainly the prettiest girl in town, but I guess she's just too old for me and too dern set in her ways."

I lacked the energy to make a suitable reply. My stomach was too empty to tolerate such feeble chatter.

Len Ramsbottom put Prudence gently into his little car and tucked an overcoat around her. He kissed her tenderly on the forehead and cheeks. She seemed reluctant to take her arms away from around his neck.

There was a noise like a concrete mixer starting up and I saw our old Dennis pull away from the kerb with Herbert crouched over the wheel.

The downpour had spent itself, but it was easy to see that the rain was not over, not by a long chalk. The sky was low and thunderous. Only one yellow gleam had penetrated the scowling pile of cloud and it lay like a path along the glistening, black bitumen of the main street right from the misty, dripping elm-tree clear along to the band rotunda. The people moved away in groups from under the shop veranda, and began to cross the street.

210

I watched a wet-through Uncle Athol wander into the Federal Hotel grinning all over his chops. The thing that made me so mad was that I knew what he was thinking. He was thinking it was going to be to his advantage to have a cop in the family. I despised that man so much it went against the grain to even think of him as my uncle. In fact I decided never to address him as "Uncle" any more. He was Ma's brother, but there, as far as I was concerned, the relationship ended.

"Athol," a voice called plaintively and Charlie Dabney waddled past. A man was plucking at his sleeve, detaining him, asking him what he was going to do about people breaking in the front door of the shop like that, but Charlie just waved him away and said something. I am not sure what he said exactly, but it sounded like "Episode closed!"